EVERY LITTLE
CROOK AND NANNY

EVERY LITTLE
CROOK AND NANNY

ED McBAIN
writing as Evan Hunter

MYSTERIOUSPRESS.COM

INTEGRATED MEDIA

NEW YORK

Copyright © by Evan Hunter

Cover design by Jason Gabbert

978-1-5040-3932-1

This 2016 edition published by MysteriousPress.com/Open Road Integrated Media, Inc.
180 Maiden Lane
New York, NY 10038
www.mysteriouspress.com
www.openroadmedia.com

THIS IS FOR VIVIAN AND JACK FARREN

EVERY LITTLE
CROOK AND NANNY

1: BENNY NAPKINS

It was a gorgeous Wednesday in August, of which there had not been too many in New York this summer. It reminded Benny Napkins of the good old days in Chicago, back in the sixties, when he had been in the garbage and linen profession. Not the winters in Chicago, no, because to tell the truth those had not been so pleasant, having to hang onto ropes tied to office buildings to keep from getting blown off Michigan Avenue, who needed *that* kind of breeziness? But he could recall Chicago summer days that inspired a man to poesy, mild summer zephyrs wafting in off the lake, guitars strumming, broads parading. Still, what good did it do to reminisce? Bygone days were bygone days. Linger on memories of summers past, and a person could miss the beauty of a truly magnificent August day that was actually here and now, the sky the color of Jeanette Kay's eyes, the trees in splendid emerald leaf awaiting the onslaught of fall.

He looked at the expectant trees through the windshield of the red Volkswagen. *I think that I shall never see,* he recited silently and completely from memory, *a poem lovely as a tree.* He pressed the accelerator to the floor and glanced simultaneously into the rearview mirror. This was not a day to get stopped by a state trooper. Not that any day, for that matter, was a day to get stopped by *anyone* connected with the Law. But especially not today. Nanny had called today, and Nanny had said there was trouble.

"What kind of trouble?" he had asked.

"Serious trouble," Nanny had replied.

"Yes, but what kind?"

"I can't tell you on the telephone."

"If you can't tell me on the telephone, why did you telephone?"

"To ask you to come here right away."

"I'm still in bed," Benny had said. "It's the middle of the night."

"It's nine-thirty in the morning."

"Jeanette Kay is still asleep. As God is my witness, Nanny, she is asleep here beside me."

"So what?"

"A man can't simply get out of bed and disappear in the middle of the night without telling his loved one that he is leaving."

"Wake her and tell her," Nanny had said.

"I don't like to do that. I like her to sleep till she's all slept out."

"Leave her a note."

"Jeanette Kay wouldn't read it."

"Why not?"

"She doesn't like to read."

"Make it a short note."

"Even if it's short."

There had been a gravid silence on the line. Then Nanny had said, in the very precise English she used whenever she wished to remind people she had come from London only two years ago, "I am certain that Mr. Ganucci, when he returns, will be interested in learning that one of his trusted fellows did not respond to a call for help from his son's governess."

There had been another long silence.

Then Benny had said, "I'll get dressed and come right over."

"Yes, please do," Nanny had replied, and hung up.

It was now ten forty-five, which meant that in just an hour and fifteen minutes, Benny had got out of bed, taken off his black silk pajamas, showered, drunk a glass of grapefruit juice and a cup of coffee, dressed in his lightweight wool-Dacron suit (with matching blue socks, striped tie, white shirt, and black shoes), run down the five flights from his apartment on Third Avenue and Twenty-fourth Street, rushed across the street to where he parked the Volkswagen in a garage owned by Ralph Rimessa, whom he had known in Chicago in the sixties when he had been in the garbage and linen profession and who consequently charged him only half the usual rate for monthly parking, and driven all the way here to (he looked for a parkway sign to tell him where he was; well, *wherever* he was, almost to Larchmont, that was for sure, which was pretty fast moving for a man as big as he was).

Not that he was big.

He was, in fact, exactly five feet eight and three-quarter inches tall. He had once tried to talk a clerk at the Motor Vehicle Bureau into putting 5'9" on his driver's license, but the clerk had been one of those namby-pamby Goody Two-shoes who insisted on doing everything by the book, even though Benny had been throwing around some pretty big figures. As a matter of fact, he *still* found it impossible to understand why that mealymouthed little clerk could not be convinced—what difference did a lousy quarter of an inch make when the sum in question was something like forty dollars? But five feet eight and three-quarter inches it had remained, and that was what he was, and that was not big.

Well, perhaps in his childhood neighborhood on Taylor Street, five feet eight and three-quarter inches might have been considered big, especially since most of the people there were immigrants from Naples, which did not boast of a particularly statuesque population (with the possible exception of Sophia Loren, who, Benny supposed, was a population unto herself). But he had not been tall as a child, either.

The only time he could have been considered big, in fact, was when he had put on thirty pounds in as many days merely because it had been necessary to sample the food in so many restaurants. In those good old days, all the fellows had called him Fat Benny Napkins. Behind his back, of course. Until one night he overheard Andy Piselli bandying the name about, and then Andy met with that unfortunate accident of his in Cicero after which all the fellows immediately began calling him plain Benny Napkins again, or Ben Napkins, which was even more dignified.

He smiled as he drove along, the sun glancing through the branches of the trees, the leaves throwing their dappled patterns onto the windshield of the small car. It was a gorgeous Wednesday, and he was delighted to be awake and about before his usual hour. On a day like today, only an ingrate could be unhappy. He quickly recited a *Hail Mary* completely from memory and simultaneously reviewed all the things that made him so happy today: He had a nice little apartment on Twenty-fourth Street, which Jeanette Kay Pezza was kind enough to share with him most of the time, not to mention a little cottage in Spotswood, New Jersey, where he grew corn so sweet it made the teeth ache; he had a 1968 Volkswagen that had never given him a minute's trouble and started up immediately even in the winter; he had a nice outdoor job that didn't demand too much of his time and that paid a decent salary; and here he was on the way to Larchmont, enjoying the beautiful day and the drive to Many Maples, where he would try to help Nanny. He was flattered that she had chosen him over all the other fellows as the person to whom she wished to talk. He enjoyed listening to her. She was a lady to the marrow, and her voice with its pleasant English lilt was as lyric as a lark's.

"The little bastard's missing," Nanny said.

They were sitting in the living room near the big marble fireplace, Ganooch's collection of clocks on the wall, and also on the mantel, and also standing to either side of the open hearth (filled with flowerpots now), all of them ticking away minutes, throwing minutes into the room like strings of firecrackers. It was almost eleven o'clock. The governess was wearing a black dress with a little white collar. Her slender hands were folded in her lap. There was a look of intense pain and bewilderment on her face.

"Let's start from the beginning," Benny said.

"That *is* the beginning."

"No, it's more like the end. When did you discover . . . ?"

"Forgive me, I'm so distraught I don't know what I'm . . ."

"There, there," Benny said.

"But he is missing, you see, and I'm all at sixes and sevens. That's why I called you."

"Well, I certainly appreciate your confi . . ."

"Instead of anyone important," Nanny said. "I figured if I called anyone important, Mr. Ganucci might find out what happened."

"Oh."

"So I figured I would call someone who is very small potatoes."

"I see."

"You were the smallest potatoes I could think of offhand."

All the clocks in the living room suddenly began tolling the hour, causing Nanny to wince, bonging and chiming and tinkling together, while unrelentingly ticking and tocking. And since it was eleven o'clock, and since presumably there would be a great deal of bonging and chiming and tinkling before they could resume their conversation, Benny seized the opportunity to reflect upon what she had just said. Yes, he had to admit he was very small potatoes as compared to some of the other fellows. Well, *most* of the other fellows. (If there was one thing Benny admired about himself, it was his uncompromising honesty.) But the fact that he was unimportant did not overly disturb him. He had once been very big in Chicago; he attributed his status now only to a little mistake he had made back in 1966. But who does not make mistakes, Benny asked himself, who indeed? The clocks continued their racket, as though clamoring to be fed. Nanny had covered her delicate ears with both hands and was now waiting for the din to subside. It did so all at once, just as it had begun. The living room was silent again, except for the incessant ticking and tocking.

"Beastly clocks," she said. "As if there isn't enough trouble in the world."

"Let's get back to *your* trouble," Benny said. "When did you discover he was missing?"

"At eight o'clock this morning. I went into his bedroom, and he wasn't there."

"Is he usually there?"

"In bed? At eight o'clock in the morning? Yes, of course he's usually there."

"But he was not there this morning."

"He was not there. And he is still not there. Nor anywhere in the house. Nor anywhere on the grounds, so far as I can tell."

"Maybe he's hiding or something," Benny suggested.

"I don't think so. He's not very playful that way. He's a rather serious little bastard."

"How old is he now, anyway?" Benny asked.

"He was ten years old last month."

"I see."

"His father gave him a watch for his birthday."

"I see."

"While at the same time paying tribute to a man he respects and admires," Nanny said.

"I see," Benny said, not wishing to pry. "I thought maybe if Lewis was slightly older, he might have a little girl friend, and maybe he went to visit her or something."

"No," Nanny said.

"No, I guess not."

"No. Lewis is missing. He is purely and simply missing. If Mr. Ganucci finds out about this . . ."

"Now, now," Benny said, "Ganooch is in Italy, I don't see how he can possibly find out about it, do you? Besides, Lewis will probably turn up any minute now and all your troubles will be over."

"I do hope so. The little bastard has me worried silly."

"My brother one time," Benny said reassuringly, "when we were both little kids in Chicago, was missing all day long. Angelo. My brother."

"Where was he?"

"Who?"

"Your brother."

"Angelo? In a garbage can, how do you like that?" Benny slapped his thigh, and burst out laughing. "He was hiding in a garbage can in the backyard! He stunk terrible when he finally came in the house."

"But he did finally come back?"

"Oh, sure. The same way little Lewis'll finally come back. You know how kids are, always looking for adventure."

"Well, Lewis isn't normally too adventurous," Nanny said.

"Even so. He probably got it in his head to take a walk or something. You got big grounds here, he may be out in the woods or something, watching ants or something. You know how kids are."

"Yes," Nanny said dubiously.

"So don't worry, everything'll be okay. Would it be all right if I used the telephone?"

"Yes, certainly. There's one in Mr. Ganucci's study."

She rose gracefully and led him out of the living room, and across the hall to where she slid open two heavily paneled doors. The study was quietly and tastefully furnished, the air redolent of good leather and musty books. Sunshine flowed through the leaded bay window at one end of the room, touching the leather-topped desk before it with a golden, mote-filled shaft of light.

"The telephone is there on Mr. Ganucci's desk," Nanny said. "I'll step out a moment, if you don't mind. The mail generally comes at eleven."

She closed the doors behind her and left Benny alone. He wandered to the bookshelves that lined one complete wall of the room, studying Ganooch's library, all of it bound in hand-tooled leather, and then turned away abruptly and went to the desk. He sat in the brown swivel chair, the leather sighing beneath him as he sank into it, reached for the phone, and quickly dialed his apartment in Manhattan. Jeanette Kay answered on the third ring.

"Hello?" she said.

"This is Benny," he said. "Were you asleep?"

"No," she said. "I got up a little while ago."

"Did you see my note?"

"What note?"

"I left a note on the refrigerator door."

"No, I didn't see it."

"Did you go to the refrigerator?"

"I'm standing right by the refrigerator this very minute," Jeanette Kay said.

"Well, do you see the note?"

"Yes, I see it. What does it say?"

"It says I'm going up to Larchmont."

"Oh. Okay. When are you going?"

"I'm here now."

"Where?"

"In Larchmont."

"Oh. I thought you said you were *going* to Larchmont."

"When I wrote the note, I wasn't here yet, I was about to *leave* for here."

"Oh," Jeanette Kay said. She hesitated a moment, and then said, "That's what I hate about reading."

"Anyway, I'll be through here soon, but I got to go to Harlem to pick up the work, so I won't be home till sometime this afternoon."

"Okay," Jeanette Kay said. "Are we going out tonight?"

"Would you like to go out tonight?"

"I don't know. What day is it?"

"It's Wednesday."

"Wednesday is *Beverly Hillbillies.*"

"No, that's Monday."

"It's Wednesday, too, Ben, don't tell me."

"Well, what do you think?"

"I'll see how I feel," she said. "They're all reruns now, anyway."

"Okay, I'll talk to you later."

"G'by," she said, and hung up. Benny replaced the receiver on the cradle, luxuriated in the feel of the leather chair for one last delicious moment, and then rose and walked swiftly to the sliding doors. He was stepping into the entrance foyer when Nanny came through the front door with the mail. Her hands were trembling.

"What is it?" Benny asked immediately.

Nanny was speechless. She handed the stack of mail to him, and he leafed through it quickly: a bill from the electric company, another from Diners' Club, a third from Lord & Taylor's, a postcard with a beautiful picture on it—

He quickly turned the card over to read it:

Benny shrugged. It was a nice enough card, well written and informative. Aside from Ganooch's promise to see Nanny at the end of the month (by which time little Lewis would most *certainly* have come out of his garbage can or wherever it was he had hidden), Benny could see nothing in it that might have so obviously upset her. Upset she was, no question about it. She stood leaning limply against the entrance door, trembling, one hand to her mouth, her eyes wide in fright. Benny looked at the last envelope in his hand. It was a strange envelope to be finding in the morning mail, primarily because there was neither a stamp nor an address on it. He lifted the flap, pulled out a sheet of writing paper, unfolded it, and read the words pasted to it:

We've got *your* SoN

We WILL RE turn him For a *mere*

$ 50,000

Get the MONEY NOW!

You will Here from US

"Oh boy," Benny said.

2: GANOOCH

On a side street off a piazza in Naples, Carmine Ganucci sat at an outdoor table with two men who were trying to explain a rather complicated business deal to him. One of the men was named Giuseppe Ladruncolo, and the other was named Massimo Truffatore. Ladruncolo was perhaps sixty-five years old, and he sported a handlebar mustache which he swept upwards with the back of his hand each time he took a sip of red wine. He was wearing a pinstripe suit and a white shirt without a tie. Truffatore was more elegantly dressed. He was a man in his forties, Ladruncolo's nephew on his mother's side, in fact, and he considered himself one of the sportiest dressers in Naples if not the entire south of Italy. (He had never been to Sicily.) Truffatore was wearing a dark brown sharkskin suit, a pale green shirt, a yellow tie, yellow socks with green clocks, and brown and white shoes. He had dark brown eyes and black hair, as had his uncle. But he was clean-shaven and his manners were meticulous; he used only his thumb and forefinger each time he lifted his wineglass to his lips.

"I'm not sure I understand the deal," Ganucci said. He did

not like the idea of having had to come into Naples when he was supposed to be on vacation. He did not much like Ladruncolo or Truffatore, but he detested Naples. His father had been born in Naples and had had the good sense to get out of here at the age of fourteen. Ladruncolo and Truffatore had been deported from America for various little activities, oh, many years back, but that did not mean they had to *choose* to live in Naples when there were so many beautiful cities in Italy. To Ganucci's mind, this qualified them as morons. Moreover, they smelled bad.

"The deal is simple," Truffatore said.

"Yes, so explain it," Ganucci said.

"We have ten thousand six hundred and sixty-five silver-plated medallions," Truffatore said. "Each weighing about three-eighths of an ounce."

"Fine," Ganucci said. "So what?"

"With a nice picture of the Virgin Mary stamped on each medallion, with her shawl done in blue enamel," Truffatore said.

"Very nice," Ganucci said.

"And we wish to ship these ten thousand six hundred and sixty-five medallions to the New York Novelty & Souvenir Company on Broadway and Forty-seventh Street."

"So ship them," Ganucci said. "There's nothing illegal about shipping silver-plated medallions to a novelty company. Moreover, the duty on such crap is probably very small. It's an entirely legal operation, so what are you wasting my time?"

"The medallions are gold," Ladruncolo said, lowering his voice.

"You said they were silver-plated."

"They are silver-plated, but underneath the silver plate is gold."

"That is a horse of another color," Ganucci said. "How much are these ten thousand six hundred and sixty-five medallions worth?"

"The going rate for gold is thirty-five dollars an ounce," Truffatore said. "Of course, we would have to discount this particular gold."

"Of course," Ganucci said. "How much are the medallions worth, after they've been discounted?"

"We are figuring that for the four thousand ounces . . ."

"Yes, yes," Ganucci said impatiently.

"Forty-nine million six hundred thousand lira, give or take."

"In American," Ganucci said. "Give or take."

"Eighty thousand dollars."

"Where'd you get this particular gold?" Ganucci asked.

"From the Banco di Napoli a month ago. We went there after twelve thousand dollars in cash, which we also got." Truffatore shrugged. "But there were ten gold bars laying around on the floor of the vault; so we picked those up, too, before we left."

"And melted them down," Ladruncolo said.

"And had the medallions cast," Truffatore said. "And now we want to send them to New York in payment."

"For what?"

"For a shipment of paste pearls that the New York Novelty & Souvenir Company ordered for us from Japan."

"That's a lot of money for a shipment of paste pearls."

"Inside the paste pearls, there is three and a half kilos of pure heroin which we plan to ship here and there after we bust them open."

"Where are the pearls now?"

"They will be arriving in Naples this Saturday. On a ship from Tokyo."

"So then," Ganucci said, "if I understand the deal correctly, you wish to ship some silver-plated medallions of the Virgin Mary inside of which . . ."

"With nice blue enameled shawls, don't forget," Truffatore said.

". . . inside of which is eighty thousand dollars in melted-down gold bullion you withdrew from the Banco di Napoli, in payment for a shipment of paste pearls which are arriving Saturday on a ship from Tokyo, inside of which is three and a half kilos of pure heroin."

"That's the picture," Ladruncolo said.

"What do you want from me?" Ganucci said.

"We wish to lay this off on you."

"How?"

"The New York Novelty & Souvenir Company is a little short of capital at the moment and can't wait for our consignment of medallions to get there. They're willing to discount the pearls, but they want cold cash or they won't release the shipment when it gets here."

"How much cash?"

"Sixty-two thousand dollars."

"That's a lot of money," Ganucci said.

"Yes, but in return for that, we'll send the shipment of Virgin Mary medallions to *you*, instead of the New York Novelty & Souvenir Company. You invest sixty-two, and when the medallions arrive in New York, you'll get back eighty. That's even better than loan sharking."

"No, it isn't," Ganucci said. "What's today?"

"Wednesday."

"And you need sixty-two by Saturday?"

"You could raise that in a minute if you had to."

"I could raise it in a minute if I was in New York."

"Gold is very easy to dispose of," Truffatore said. "Wash off the silver plate, melt the stuff down, and you get rid of it anyplace in the country. There ain't a soul in the world could tell it was hot."

"That's true," Ganucci said.

"And your profit is eighteen thousand dollars."

"True," Ganucci said. "The deal is maybe all right. It's raising the money that bothers me. I'm not right on the scene, you know. I'm here in Italy."

"Al Capone used to run things from Alcatraz."

"There are not many men like Al Capone left," Ganucci said, and lowered his eyes in respect.

"True, but the fellows say good things about you, too," Ladruncolo said.

"Sixty-two thousand dollars," Ganucci said, and shook his head.

"Look at it this way," Truffatore said. "I understand that you have invested in Broadway shows on occasion. Well, this is safer than a Broadway show."

"I *have* invested in one or two Broadway shows," Ganucci said, "but only because my wife Stella was once in show business and has a soft spot in her heart for the profession."

"What do you think?" Truffatore said.

"I think I *may* be able to raise the money by Saturday morning."

"Good, then . . ."

"Provided," Ganucci said.

Truffatore looked at Ladruncolo.

"Provided *what*?" Ladruncolo asked.

"The discount is improved."

"By how much?"

"You mentioned that you also picked up twelve thousand dollars in cash when you knocked off the bank. Deduct that from the sixty-two thousand, and we've got a deal."

"That money is long since gone."

"When did you say the bank was kicked over?"

"Last month."

"That money is still hot, and therefore it is *not* long since gone," Ganucci said. "I'll deliver fifty thousand dollars to you on Saturday morning, in return for your shipment of Virgin

Mary medallions guaranteed to be worth eighty thousand dollars. That's the deal. And I mean *guaranteed.* I don't have to tell
you what'll happen if those medallions turn out to be *really* silver plate."

"They're solid gold, don't worry about that."

"Yes or no?" Ganucci said.

"You're asking for too big a profit," Truffatore protested.

"Yes or no?" Ganucci said. "Is it a deal?"

"It's a deal," Ladruncolo said.

"It's a deal," Truffatore said glumly.

Stella Ganucci loved the sun.

She attributed this to the fact that during her show business
days she had never been allowed to go out in the sun. Stella was
a big lady, five feet nine inches tall, with blond hair and blue
eyes and a fair complexion. She had been told time and again,
back in the old show business days, that audiences did not appreciate looking at a big job who was lobster red from the sun.
This, of course, was when she used to perform in Miami. She
had insisted that she could cover herself all over with powder,
which was what she did, anyway. But the edict had held: no sun
for Stella.

She had once asked Mr. Padrone, who ran the club on Collins Avenue, "Mr. Padrone, why can there never be sun for sun
nor star for star?" and Mr. Padrone had said, "What the hell are
you talking about?" and that had been the end of the argument.
Stella had known what she was talking about. Stella always
knew what she was talking about. She had been talking about
stella, which meant star, and star meant sun, and it seemed terribly unfair to her and not a little uncompromising that there
could never be sun for sun nor star for star, *that* was what she'd
been talking about, of course.

She luxuriated now in the late afternoon sunshine at the

pool of the Quisisana Hotel on Capri, and wondered why people never understood her. It seemed to Stella that she was perfectly understandable. Except here, of course, because she did not speak a word of Italian. Well, not *here*, exactly, not *here* poolside at the Quisisana because every person here was American, and the only ones who spoke Italian were beachboys and busboys and waiters, and Carmine would have busted her head if she'd opened her mouth to any of them. Carmine was very peculiar that way. Still, he did understand her. Most of the time.

Nanny did *not* understand her most of the time. Nanny, in fact, *never* understood her, which made it difficult. The misunderstanding had started almost at once because Stella could not honestly see why they needed a governess for an eight-year-old child.

"To teach him things," Carmine had said.

"What sort of things?"

"Culture."

"I can teach him culture by myself."

"I know you can," Carmine said, "but can you teach him *English* culture?"

"Culture is culture," Stella said.

"She's a good governess," Carmine replied. "Let's give it a try."

Nanny had moved into the house two years ago, to occupy what had once been a large storage room on the second floor, down the corridor from Carmine's darkroom. To tell the truth, Stella couldn't see much change in Lewis. To her, he looked about as cultured as he had always looked. She had to admit that Nanny added a certain tone to the household, what with her nice manners, and her pleasant English accent, but it was also a trial having her around all the time, like not being able to say "Shit" when she wanted to—things like that. Stella rarely used profanity (Carmine would have busted her head if she did), but occasionally she used a dirty word or two when she thought she was alone. With Nanny around the house all the time, she was hardly ever alone.

She was hardly ever alone at the pool of the Quisisana, either, but that didn't bother her too much, mainly because she would never dream of using profanity in public.

"Did your husband take the helicopter to Naples?" Marcia Leavitt asked.

Marcia was wearing a bikini she had bought in St. Tropez the week before. She was a trim little brunette with tiny breasts; she would never have made it in Miami, Stella thought, and then said, "Yes, he took the helicopter."

"Does he like that city?" Marcia asked.

"No," Stella said, "he doesn't, really."

"I *hate* that city," Marcia said.

"I don't believe Carmine cares for it too much, either," Stella said.

"That's my least favorite city in the whole world," Marcia said.

"My husband doesn't like it, either."

"I detest that city," Marcia said. "'See Naples and die' is right. You *could* die from Naples."

"My husband . . ."

"I abhor that city," Marcia said. "What does your husband find so attractive in that damn city? Does he have business there?"

"No, he's retired," Stella said.

"Oh? What line did he used to be in?"

"Soft drinks. He's a retired soft drinks manufacturer," Stella said.

"Oh, really? Would I know the soft drink he manufactured?"

"I don't think so. It was sold only in the Midwest."

"It's not Pepsi-Cola or anything like that?"

"No."

"Or Coca-Cola?"

"No."

"Where in the Midwest?"

"Chicago mostly."

"I'm not too familiar with Chicago," Marcia said, and rolled over on her belly. She undid the straps on her bikini top, closed her eyes, let out a deep sigh, and said, "I'm from Los Angeles myself."

Stella did not answer. She had once played Los Angeles on the same bill with Sandy Rowles, who at that time was living with a fellow named Dan Birraio. Birraio had been Carmine's partner back in the old days in Chicago when they were both making beer. From what Stella understood, they had made very *good* beer, which was quite considerate of them since they really didn't have to. But if there was one thing Carmine believed in, it was quality. Never mind the expense involved, he had always insisted on the best malts and hops, whatever they were. Sandy had once told Stella that Birraio wore a gun to bed. When Stella in turn reported this to Carmine, to whom she was not yet married, he had said simply, "That fellow has no manners." Which was true. In all the time she had known Carmine, he had never once worn a gun to bed. Well, only once. But that was a special occasion following his sister's wedding, when they were expecting trouble from the fellows in Brooklyn. And the gun had only been a tiny little one strapped to his leg just above his garter. And actually, he'd forgotten to take it off when he climbed into bed only because he had drunk too much at Theresa's wedding when it was learned that the fellows in Brooklyn had met with an unfortunate accident after somebody threw a bomb in the candy store where they hung out.

She missed little Lewis.

Suddenly—with the scent of suntan lotion rising from Marcia Leavitt's back, and the sound of muffled voices drifting over the sparkling water of the pool, the muted Italian of beachboys talking to busboys, the sound of silverware clinking, a jet droning overhead against the pristine sky—suddenly she missed her ten-year-old son with a desperation she had not felt since the first time she stepped onto the stage at the old Triboro Theater on 125th Street, a slip of a sixteen-year-old girl with enormous tits even then, and the lights went out on cue, and she discovered that her G-string wasn't fluorescent as the manager had promised her, and nobody could see her spectacular grinds in the dark. Carmine had later visited the manager in the hospital and brought him a dozen roses after he had his terrible fall from the top of the second balcony.

She sure missed her son.

Maybe she could talk Carmine into cutting the trip short and taking her home.

Like maybe tomorrow.

3: LUTHER

Luther Patterson talked out loud to himself much of the time, but that was only because his wife, Ida, was such a quiet woman. Ida was quiet because she was never quite certain whether Luther was addressing her or Simon or Levin. Luther's admiration and respect for Simon and Levin knew no bounds, and most of his external monologues were addressed to one or both of those giants. Much of Luther's waking day, in fact, was spent either in solitary dialogue with Simon and Levin or else in trying to figure out how either of them would react to any situation then confronting Luther.

Simon and Levin were not male vocalists. (Once in a while, when Luther was feeling exceptionally musical, he did address a discourse or two to Simon and Garfunkel, but they were quite two different cups of tea.) Simon and Levin were only perhaps the two greatest living critics, dead or alive, in the United States of America.

If there were two things Luther Patterson aspired to be, they were both Simon and Levin. Whenever he thought of the unique combination of bile and style that both men possessed, he felt totally inadequate in his chosen profession, and not a trifle envious besides. Several months back, he had begun two separate scrapbooks, one of *The Collected Works of John Simon,* and the other of *The Collected Works of Martin Levin.* He studied these scrapbooks for hours on end, trying to absorb the unique quality both men brought to their work, the essence of which spelled greatness. On occasion, he entertained the bizarre notion that Martin Levin and John Simon were actually one and the same person. Had they ever, for example, been seen together on the same television show? If Martin Levin was not really a person inside John Simon clamoring to be let out, or vice versa, then how did one account for the identical precise, literate, informative, scrupulous, meticulous, painstaking, scholarly, incisive, penetrating, probing, resonant, intensely felt nature of their separate reviews and critical essays?

"Tell me, John Simon, are you really Martin Levin?" Luther shouted.

Ida, who knew right off he was not addressing her, did not answer him.

"I thought not," Luther said. "That would be the same as claiming Shakespeare and Marlowe were one and the same. Why can't people accept the fact that two literary phenomena can be contemporaries, working and reacting to the same environment in equally beautiful and sensitive ways without each being the other or vice versa? I ask you, Martin Levin."

God, if only I could write like you, he thought, and went to his bookshelf and took down *The Collected Works of Martin Levin,* and scanned the clippings, trying to pick up little hints that might help him in his own critical forays. Expressions like "disappointingly tedious" sprang from the text, "has made his hero odious without making him interesting," wonderful, wonderful. Or "The novel plods along at the same underpowered dramatic level," oh God, to be able to put words together that way. In a near frenzy of ecstasy, Luther pulled down the companion volume of clippings, *The Collected Works of John Simon*, turning to a review at random (they were all so exquisitely composed, it hardly mattered where a person's eye fell, the delight of absorbing true creativity was invariably his reward), and read aloud:

> Let our youthful rebels beware: social and political commitment without commitment to articulateness and poetry will do little for the world beyond transforming it into a monstrous discothèque, free and equally brutalizing to all.

The words echoed in Luther Patterson's high-ceilinged living room, "free and equally brutalizing to all," a phrase that John Simon himself, were he not most certainly a modest man, might have emblazoned on his shield as a motto of sorts—"Free and Equally Brutalizing To All," lapis on azure perhaps, with two gules pendant.

In a burst of familiarity, Luther called out, "Johnny, what do you think of that idea?" Receiving no reply, he replaced both cherished volumes on the shelf and went into the kitchen, where Ida was preparing lunch. He lifted the cover of the pot on the rear burner of the stove, picked up a tasting spoon, glanced at the ceiling again, and said, "John Simon, do you know I have a doctorate in comparative literature from Princeton University, do you realize that, John? Do you know that I was graduated *summa cum laude,* Phi Beta Kappa, third in my class? John Baby, let's have a drink together one day—after I've collected, of course, after this is over and done with—sit together in the salon on my yacht and exchange literary bons mots, how I'd enjoy that, how I would truly enjoy that." He put the cover back on the pot, and the spoon on the stove top. Then, because he was a critic, he said, "This soup stinks," and went back into the living room.

If there was one thing Luther Patterson possessed, it was an enormous library. The one reason he had taken this huge tenth-floor apartment on West End Avenue (besides the cheap rent) was that it had a living room almost as long as a bowling alley, the length of which was covered from floor to ceiling with bookshelves, which in turn supported hundreds and hundreds of books, all of which Luther had carefully read and evaluated. Luther got the books free. He also got paid to read and evaluate them. He did not enjoy reading too much, but then, who did? In that one respect, he was truly envious of his colleague John Simon (he dared to whisper the word "colleague" only in the privacy of his own mind, as though sacrilegiously linking his own name with that of, say, George Bernard Shaw or William Jennings Bryan). Simon not only reviewed books, he also had the opportunity of seeing a lot of plays and movies free before expressing his carefully considered opinions. That was a very nice aspect of the profession, Luther thought. *Simon's* profession, not his. Luther reviewed only books. Always books. For unimportant journals and obscure publications. Books all the goddamn time. The only way *he* ever got to see a play free was to sneak in during the intermission and then look around in the dark for an empty seat. He never did this when he was with Ida. Ida disliked dishonesty of any sort. She wasn't even too keen on his having kidnaped Lewis Ganucci.

Luther sat in his high-ceilinged, book-lined living room overlooking West End Avenue, tapped the balls of his fingers ever so lightly together, and wondered how the Ganucci lad was doing. He had locked the son of the retired soft drinks magnate in the back bedroom of the apartment, where any cries for help would register only on the blank brick wall of the adjacent building. He had then driven back to Larchmont in his

1963 hardtop Chevrolet and put the ransom note in Carmine Ganucci's mailbox. He had felt a thrill of accomplishment as he slid the envelope in with the morning mail. Not the same thrill he had felt while composing the note, of course, nor even the same thrill he had experienced when stealing into the millionaire's mansion last night and clapping his hand over the boy's mouth and spiriting him away; no, that had really been quite exciting.

"It was *really* exciting, Martin," he said aloud. "*Vraiment émouvant*, if you take my meaning."

In fact (and he had to admit this because if there was one thing Luther admired about himself, it was his uncompromising honesty), the Ganucci grounds and house had been the *most* exciting part of the entire adventure. He had never been to a place as exuberantly gauche as the Ganucci homestead, but then what could one expect of a man who had made his fortune bottling and selling soft drinks in the Midwest? To each his own, certainly, but there was hardly anything creative about such a pursuit, and Luther should not have been surprised to find the millionaire's mansion a baroque monstrosity that dominated acres of rolling green lawn and . . .

"How would *you* put that, John?" Luther asked aloud. "Virid mead? *Hát nézd, tulajdonképp nem számít*, John," he said, lapsing into Hungarian. "*A stílusod kifogástalan, a képeid érzékletesek, a kritikai érzéked megtámadhatatlan.*"

But the amazing thing about his response to the ugly old house was that he had been overwhelmed by the sheer luxury of it, the heady scent of moneyed exclusivity almost causing him to become dizzy as he pried open the sleeping lad's window. All during the abduction, he experienced this same sort of giddy awareness of immense wealth, heightened by the knowledge that at least *some* of that wealth would soon accrue to him. Before he had stolen onto the grounds past the dozens of maples that stood like leafy sentinels (Nice, he thought, well put, Luther) on the lawn in front of Ganucci's architectural horror, he had thought of asking no more than ten thousand dollars for the safe return of the boy. But on the way back to Manhattan, he had been unable to dispel the scent, the stink, the stench of millions and millions of dollars earned, for Christ's sake, by bottling soft drinks when a truly creative person like himself strained so hard to earn the meanest living. It was then that he decided to raise the ante to twenty thousand dollars; his weeks of careful research were at least worth that much. By the time he got back to the West End Avenue apartment, however, the smell of money was so overpowering that he had to revise his note three more times, escalating the demand in ten-thousand-dollar jumps until he reached his final draft, wherein he set the ransom at $50,000.

His approach had been unorthodox, to say the least. He had first looked for an estate that appeared as though it might support the kind of family he hoped to victimize. (Well, victimize was perhaps too strong a word. It had never entered his head until this moment, as a matter of fact, and he rejected it at once. He intended no harm to the boy. All he expected was some reasonable recompense for his labor.) He had found Many Maples quite by chance, having drawn on an Esso map a circle with a radius of twenty-five miles, its center being New York City. He had explored Lower Westchester like a latter-day Richbell. Many Maples seemed perfect. Moreover, his discreet inquiries in town, at shops and gasoline stations, restaurants and cocktail lounges, boutiques and haberdasheries, garnered for him the information that Carmine Ganucci was one of the wealthiest men in the small community, a respected member of the school board and head of the Lions Club Ambulance Corps. But what interested Luther most was the fact that Carmine Ganucci had a ten-year-old son named Lewis.

The thing to do now (well perhaps not this instant, but certainly after lunch sometime—if he could get through soup) was to call the Ganucci mansion and ask them if they had got the money together. He would then say they would be contacted again to let them know when and where he wished the money delivered.

Luther was feeling good.

"I think I'll have a drink, John, Martin, what do you say?" he asked aloud. He went to the bar opposite the bookcase and began mixing himself a very strong martini. The way he looked at it (and this was what made him feel so good), if he couldn't be as successful a critic as Simon or Levin, he could certainly be a successful kidnaper instead.

And that was most assuredly the next best thing.

4: THE CORSICAN BROTHERS

It was almost three P.M. before Benny got downtown to Forty-second Street.

He had left Many Maples at noon, and then had driven to Harlem to pick up the work, which had taken longer than he'd expected because a man insisted he had put fifty cents on number 311 yesterday and that was the number that had come in, whereas Benny had the word of the collector himself that the number played was 307, *not* 311, a common enough mistake, seven-eleven being the ritual chant of dice players and gamblers everywhere.

The number, of course, had only been written down a half-hour after the bet was placed, it being the habit of policemen (suspicious by nature) to assume automatically that if a man had several dozen policy slips in his pocket, he was engaged in the policy or numbers racket. The bet had been placed by Walter Anziano, a nice enough old man in his seventies, who had been playing the numbers since he first arrived in America from Palermo fifty-three years ago, fifty cents a day every day of the week, and who had hit only once in all that time, for the amazing sum of three hundred dollars.

Benny did not like to lose a steady customer like Walter Anziano. So he told the old man that there had apparently been some mixup, but that a check of yesterday's work had revealed a slip of paper in the collector's handwriting with the numerals 307-50 on it, meaning that Anziano had bet fifty cents on 307, *not* 311. The collector claimed he had written down the number as soon as he'd got off the street, and that he was certain Anziano had said 307, so it was now a matter of the collector's word against Anziano's. In any event, Benny informed the old man that they could not pay off. However, Benny was willing to give Anziano a free fifty-cent ride every day for the next week, if only to show the good will of himself and his fellows, an offer the old man grudgingly accepted only after having been plied with four shots of Four Roses in a local bar. It had been the entertainment of Walter Anziano that had occupied most of the afternoon, while little Lewis was in the hands of some cheap hoods who were undoubtedly maniacs or worse. Benny could not think of anyone but maniacs kidnaping the son of Carmine Ganucci.

He had agreed with Nanny that the matter should not come to Ganooch's attention in any way, manner, or form, because whereas it was nice weather for swimming, it would be difficult indeed to effect a splendid crawl while wearing cement blocks. The best way to keep the matter from Ganooch was to make certain that none of the fellows higher up found out about it. And the best way to make certain of that was to pay those crazy maniacs the fifty grand at once. Which was why Benny was so anxious to talk to the Corsican Brothers.

Vinny and Alfred were just beginning their famous amazing dancing doll act when Benny finally caught up with them. Alfred, the younger of the twins by fourteen hours, winked at him as he approached, and then launched into his monologue, the prelude to a choreographic masterpiece.

"Now, ladies and gentlemen," he said, "I know you are all hurrying home to your loved ones after a hard day's work, but if you'll grant me just a minute of your time, I think I can show you something wonderful to bring home to the wife or kiddies. I have here in this carton you see here at my feet, a limited amount of amazing dancing dolls which cost only fifty cents each and which when you see them perform I am sure you will agree are worth ten times that amount. There are no mechanical parts on these dolls, they are easily folded for carrying in pocket or purse, and they will continue to delight your loved ones, friends, neighbors, and all and sundry who witness their remarkable performance. If I can have one moment more of your valuable time, I am going to take one of these amazing dancing dolls out of the box here and show you what it can do."

The stage upon which the Corsican Brothers worked was a stretch of sidewalk some four feet long and three feet wide, their backdrop a brick wall darkened by the soot of centuries. An audience composed of summer out-of-town visitors, shoppers, and cinema buffs (who had wandered over from the twenty-five-cent peepshow displays slightly farther west), some two dozen people in all, watched as Alfred reached into the box. Benny stood to the left of the crowd, also watching. To the right of the crowd, standing almost against the brick wall, his hands in his pockets, stood Vinny, the star performer in the amazing dancing doll act, but a performer who sought neither applause nor recognition, a performer whose role necessitated that he remain absolutely silent, anonymous, and practically invisible. Standing directly opposite Alfred and the cardboard box that contained the amazing dancing dolls, Vinny watched like any other curious member of the audience, his hands in his pockets.

"Now this may look to you like just an ordinary doll made of cardboard and flimsy paper," Alfred said to the crowd. "In fact, as you can see, the head here *is* made of cardboard, as are the hands and the feet, and the arms and legs are just this flimsy accordion-pleated paper, practically tissue paper, you may wonder how this doll can do what it is about to do. That is the amazing thing about this doll. This doll, which is only sixteen inches tall from the top of its head to the tips of its toes, is going to dance. *I* can make it dance, *you* can make it dance, and it will continue to dance for hours and hours without ever needing recharging or replacement of parts because there are no batteries in this amazing dancing doll (how *could* there be when the whole thing is made out of paper and cardboard) and there are no mechanical parts to wear out or break. It is paper and cardboard, that is all, but the paper is specially treated so that it gathers electric ions from the very air you and I, all of us, are breathing all around us. And once those ions are gathered and stored in these flimsy little legs, why the amazing dancing doll can hardly stand still with excitement, it just begins dancing all over the place for hours on end. I'm going to show you in a minute how this little doll dances, but I want to explain first that the reason we can offer it at the low price of fifty cents is that the doll *is* made out of just this flimsy paper and cardboard, as you can see, and that's practically what it costs to manufacture and ship, with a very small markup for profit. The electric ions in the air are free and, as you all know, it is the power source that causes most prices to soar and become a burden on the consumer. Not so with this amazing dancing doll. Now let me show you."

Alfred, holding the doll by the top of its cardboard head, bent over so that the dangling cardboard feet on their accordion-pleated paper legs were almost touching the sidewalk. He shook the doll vigorously. He shook it again, even more vigorously.

"I am gathering in the electric ions," he said.

He shook the doll again.

"One, two, three shakes, sometimes a few more depending on weather conditions," he said, "that is all it takes to store the energy and set the thing in motion. Now watch."

He released the top of the doll's head. The doll began to bounce. Unsupported by Alfred, who backed away from it, the doll began to jiggle and jump on its flimsy paper legs, up and down, up and down, as though dancing for joy now that it had been infused with all those marvelous life-giving electric ions, free in the air for all to breathe. What the crowd did not see (because the brick wall backdrop was so filthy with soot) was the slender black thread stretching tight from the rim of the carton to where Vinny stood across the sidewalk, silently watching the performance albeit a performer himself. The taut black thread went directly into Vinny's pocket, where it was wrapped around the forefinger of his right hand. As Vinny jiggled his forefinger, the black thread simultaneously jiggled, and as the thread jiggled, so did the doll because what Alfred had really been doing (while earlier shaking out the doll to gather in all those electric ions) was hanging it onto the thread from a tiny hook on the back of the cardboard head. As the crowd watched goggle-eyed now, Alfred picked up the doll and said, "Who'll buy the first one, ladies and gentlemen? They're only fifty cents each, who'll buy the first one, there is only a limited supply."

A sucker in the audience (there are suckers in every audience, Benny mused silently) asked the anticipated sucker question.

"How do we know *all* the dolls can dance and not just that one doll there?"

"They can all dance," Alfred answered, "because they have all been specially treated with the ion-attracting matter. Would one of you people here just reach into the box and hand me *any* doll that's in there. There's nothing special about this particular doll, believe me. They are *all* of them exactly alike, they are all amazing. Madam, would you please do us the favor?" he said, turning to an old woman who looked like a minister's wife, but who may very well have been a retired prostitute. It made no matter; Alfred truly did not know her, and his claim that *all* of the dolls were exactly alike was a valid, honest, and legitimate one. The old lady gingerly picked a doll from the box at random.

"Now please shake it out for me, madam, just as you saw me do with the other doll," Alfred said.

The old lady shook out the doll.

"Again, please, a little harder. Thank you. And here, sir," he said to the man who had raised the question, "you give it a few shakes, too. Madam, may I, please?" He took the doll from the old lady, and handed it to the man. The man studied the doll with the scrutiny of Geppetto, gave it two vigorous shakes, and handed it back to Alfred, who immediately bent low, smiled at the crowd, and said, "Few more shakes for good measure," as he swiftly hooked it onto the black thread that ran arrow-straight into his brother Vinny's pocket. Alfred released the doll, and lo and behold, the cunning little darling began jiggling and bouncing and dancing its little heart out! Any skeptic in the crowd was immediately convinced. Common sense stridently warned that a paper and cardboard doll could not defy the laws of gravity in such a manner, even if it were specially treated with monosodium glutamate or aluminum chloral hydrate. But an old lady and a disbeliever, both as honest as the day was long, had each shaken the doll and passed it back to Alfred, who did nothing more than shake it again and set it on its feet—and now look at the damn thing dancing! Dollar bills appeared in anxious fists. Alfred busily began making change and dispensing dolls from the carton as Vinny's forefinger twitched and the doll on the unseen black thread danced its way to fame and glory. In less than five minutes, Alfred had sold fourteen of the dolls, for an almost pure profit of seven dollars. He might have gone on to

sell another dozen to the growing crowd had not Vinny emit-
ted a low whistle at that point, the signal that the cop on the
beat was approaching. Alfred snatched up the amazing dancing
doll in the middle of one of its more complicated entrechats,
tossed it into the carton, said, "Good night, folks, thank you,"
and bolted off after his brother, who hastily left behind him on
the sidewalk a broken cotton thread, his only invisible means
of support.

"You fellows are getting better all the time," Benny told them
some ten minutes later, in a cafeteria on Forty-sixth Street and
Eighth Avenue. "That was a truly remarkable performance."

"Well, thank you," Alfred said shyly, and ducked his head.

"Thank you," Vinny repeated.

"Remarkable," Benny said. "And what's even *more* remarkable is that you get away with it."

"How do you mean?" Alfred asked.

"That the people watching you don't realize you're in some
way related to each other."

"How do you mean?" Vinny asked.

"In that you look so much alike."

"Oh," Alfred said.

"Being twins, I mean."

"Oh," Vinny said.

"Identical twins," Benny said.

"Well," Alfred said, "we don't think of ourselves as twins,
you see."

"You don't?"

"No," Vinny said. "We were born fourteen hours apart."

"That's hardly twins," Alfred said.

"That's a medical phenomenon," Vinny said, "but it's not
twins."

"I thought it was twins," Benny said.

"Millie the Midwife didn't think so," Vinny said. "In fact, *she* thought her work was done. My mother thought so too. Millie went to a movie after she delivered me. That was at seven o'clock at night. She went to see *Where the Sidewalk Ends,* with Dana Andrews and Gene Tierney."

"That was a very good picture," Benny said.

"Yes, I myself saw it on television only last week," Vinny said. "Jeanette Kay watched it too."

"How *is* Jeanette Kay?" Vinny asked.

"She's fine, thank you."

"Anyway, the next morning my mother called Millie and said she was feeling very strange. 'Very strange *how?*' Millie wanted to know. My mother said she felt as if there was still somebody inside her kicking around. Millie rushed right over and they did the *malocchio.* Do you know what the *malocchio* is?"

"Yes, it's the Evil Eye," Benny said.

"Correct," Vinny said. "What Millie the Midwife done was put a few drops of oil in a dish of water. If the oil separated into drops close together, like *eyes,* that meant somebody had put the *malocchio* on my mother. Which could have accounted for why she was still feeling somebody kicking around inside there when I was already born."

"But it wasn't the *malocchio,*" Alfred said.

"Correct. The oil just lay there in the dish like a big gold coin. No eyes, nothing. So Millie said to my mother, 'Well, let's take another look, Fanny.' So they took another look, and it was Alfred."

"Me," Alfred said.

"A medical phenomenon," Vinny said.

"But not twins," Alfred said.

"How can you be sure you're not twins, though?" Benny asked.

"If we were twins, would they call us the Corsican *Brothers?* They'd call us the Corsican *Twins,* correct?"

"But the Corsican Brothers *were* twins."

"Correct," Vinny said. "But we're not. In fact, we're not even from Corsica. None of our family's from Corsica, neither. The whole thing's an entire mystery."

"The way I figure it," Alfred said, "my mother conceived twice."

"Probably with my father both times," Vinny said.

"But fourteen hours apart," Alfred said.

"That would explain it, all right," Benny said.

"That's very definitely what probably happened," Alfred said.

"So you see there's nothing remarkable about our act in *that* respect. People accept us for what we are. After all, superficial similarities don't mean nothing when there's two distinct and definite personalities involved. We're very different people, Ben."

"I'm sure you are."

"Though very much alike in many respects as well."

"But different," Alfred said.

"Different but the same," Vinny said.

"Of course the same, but different," Alfred said.

"For example," Vinny said, "whereas I've been doing a lot of talking here, I'm very shy when it comes to performing. It's Alfred who gives the spiel, you may have noticed."

"Yes, I did notice that," Benny said.

"Whereas, on the other hand," Vinny said, "I can't even draw a straight line, whereas Alfred is very talented artistically."

"Which is exactly why I came to see you."

"Why's that?" Alfred asked.

"I need fifty thousand dollars in phony bills."

"I have given up that career," Alfred said.

"You have?" Benny asked. "Why?"

"Well, I'll tell you," Alfred said. "The first batch I done was ten-dollar bills. But the fellows who went out to pass them got caught right off the bat and are now serving ten years each and respectively at Sing Sing."

"That's a shame," Benny said. "What happened?"

"I made a mistake," Alfred said. "I was working on two batches at the same time, a five-dollar batch and a ten-dollar batch. I accidentally put Lincoln's picture on the ten-dollar bills."

"We all make mistakes," Benny said.

"That's what the fellows said when I went up to visit them."

"But I'm sorry to hear this. I was hoping you could help me."

"I don't even have my equipment no more," Alfred said. "I sold the press and everything a long time ago."

"To who?"

"To Cockeye Di Strabismo."

"Why don't you try *him*?" Vinny suggested. "I'll bet he can help you."

"Yes, maybe," Benny said. "In the meantime, if you hear of any loose money that's around for sale cheap, will you get in touch with me?"

"May I ask why you need this kind of cash?" Vinny said. "Or is that too personal?"

"There has been a child snatched," Benny said.

"Which child?"

"Ganooch's son."

"Who would do a crazy thing like that?" Alfred asked.

"Listen to me," the voice on the telephone said.

"Yes?" Nanny said.

"Do you know who this is?"

"No, who is this?"

"This is the kidnaper. Who is this?"

"This is Nanny. The child's governess."

"Madam, let me talk to Mr. Ganucci at once."

"Mr. Ganucci isn't in right now."

"Where is he?"

"He's out of town," Nanny said.

"Oh, the old out-of-town trick, eh?" the voice said. "*Where* out of town?"

"In Italy."

"*Dove in Italia?*" the voice asked. "I speak seven languages fluently, don't try any more tricks."

"He's on the Isle of Capri."

"Nonsense! Put him on right this minute or we'll dispose of the child!"

"No, please," Nanny said, "I swear he's . . ."

"I've got a vicious Doberman pinscher poised to spring at that boy's throat if I give the signal. All I have to do is yell, '*Töte ihn!*' Now stop playing games and put Mr. Ganucci on the phone."

"I told you, he's in Italy."

"Madam . . ."

"Please, we're trying to get the money now. All we need is a little time."

"Who's *we*?" the voice asked. "Have you told the police about this?"

"No," Nanny said in alarm. "Have *you*?"

"Have I what? Told the police? Are you crazy, madam?"

"Forgive me, I . . ."

"Listen and listen hard," the voice said. "I'm giving you until tomorrow afternoon at five o'clock to raise the money. I'll contact you at that time and tell you where and when and how I want delivery made. Would you like some advice, madam?"

"Please," Nanny said.

"I suggest you cable Mr. Ganucci on the Isle of Capri and tell him to come home fast!"

5: COCKEYE

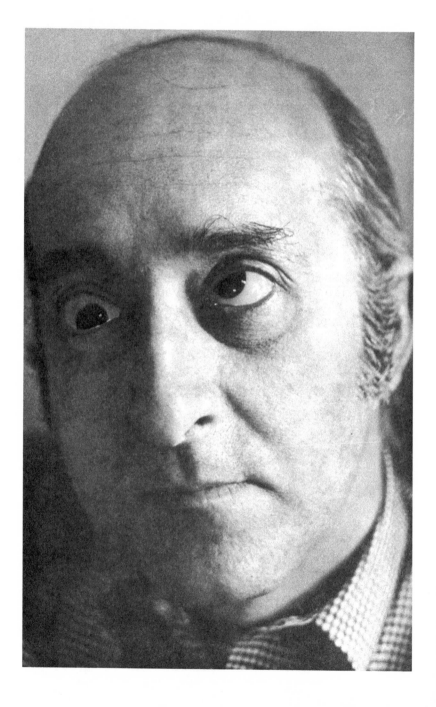

"Who is it?" a voice said.

"It is I, Benny Napkins."

"Just a second," the voice said. A flap in the door flew open. Cockeye's best eye appeared in the revealed circle. The flap dropped into place again. Benny heard the lock being turned, the night chain being taken off. The door opened.

"How you doing, Ben?" Cockeye said.

"We have a problem," Benny answered immediately.

He stepped into the loft, and Cockeye locked and chained the door behind him. The loft was immense. It had until recently been occupied by a sculptor whose latest project had been modeling parts of the human body in larger than life-size scale. When he'd moved out, he had left behind some of his earlier experimental work, and as a result the loft was crowded with enormous noses of every shape—hooked, pug, straight, flat, aquiline, broken, bobbed, and bulbous. Nose flaps gaped from ceiling and wall, bridges thrust from pedestals, nostrils lay in plaster heaps on the floor. As they picked their way through the remnants overhead and underfoot, Benny had the distinct impression that someone was breathing down his neck. He was relieved when they reached the rear of the loft, where Cockeye's printing press stood alongside the metal table on which he did his engraving. Opposite that, in a nook formed by the peculiar architecture of the loft, Cockeye had set an old sofa and a scarred coffee table. A hot plate rested on a long shelf overhung by a huge sculpture of what surely had to be the ugliest nose in the entire world.

"Is that all this guy ever made?" Benny asked. "Noses?"

"He done belly buttons, too," Cockeye said. "But he took them with him when he moved." Cockeye paused. "Well, no, he left one hanging in the bathroom."

"What was the idea?"

"I don't know," Cockeye said, and shrugged. "I guess he was maybe going to put them all together one day and have this very large statue."

Benny looked up at the nose again.

"You recognize that nose?" Cockeye asked.

"No," Benny said. "Whose nose is that?"

"Snitch's."

"You're kidding me."

"I'm serious. Snitch was up here one day sniffing around, you know, as is his habit. This was before this artist guy was all moved out, he was still running around picking up belly buttons and things. He takes one look at Snitch's nose and a light bulb goes on over his head. 'I got to do your nose!' he yells. So he gives Snitch five bucks just to sit here on a stool with his nose in the air." Cockeye looked up at the nose. "You didn't recognize it, huh?"

"No, not in that size," Benny said.

"It's the proportions in life that render things meaningful," Cockeye said, solemnly studying the nose. "You want some coffee?"

"I could use a cup, thank you," Benny said.

Cockeye went to the hot plate and set a kettle on it. "It's instant, is that all right?"

"Yes, that's fine."

"Well, what brings you here?" Cockeye asked congenially, leaning on the engraving table.

"I need fifty thousand dollars," Benny said.

"That's a large order," Cockeye answered. "How soon do you need it?"

"Immediately."

"In what denominations?"

"It wasn't specified. Small bills, I would guess. That's the usual demand."

"Who's placing this order?" Cockeye asked.

"I don't know the name of the party."

"One of our fellows?"

"I wouldn't think so."

"Because I could maybe give a larger discount if it was one of our own fellows, you understand."

"What are you currently getting for fifty thousand dollars in small denominations?" Benny asked.

"One-tenth of one per cent," Cockeye said, "or exactly fifty bucks." He paused. "Depending on the risk. If there's a higher element of risk, my percentage is perforce higher." He paused again. "May I ask to what use this money will be put?"

"It will be used to pay a ransom demand."

"Oh-ho," Cockeye said. "And who's been snatched, may I ask?"

"Carmine Ganucci's son."

Cockeye's mouth fell open.

"Uh-huh," Benny said.

"Ganooch's son?" Cockeye said, appalled.

"The very same."

"Who would do a crazy thing like that?"

"Some crazy person, who do you think?" Benny said, and rose from the couch and began pacing back and forth near the printing press. "Ganooch is in Italy right now, thank God. If we can get the kid back before he hears anything about . . ."

"Ben, I'm not so sure I want to get involved in anything that has to do with Ganooch's son."

"You *are* involved," Benny said.

"Involved? Me? How?"

"Because I came to you. Nanny came to me this morning . . ."

"Oh, Nanny, huh?" Cockeye said.

"Yes, Nanny. She came to me, which is how *I* got involved. Now I'm coming to you and that's how *you're* involved. If God forbid something should happen to Ganooch's son . . ."

"God forbid," Cockeye said, and rolled his best eye heavenward.

". . . anybody who was involved will wish he was not, I can tell you that."

"I *already* wish I was not," Cockeye said.

"Yes, so do I," Benny said, "but that's one of life's little ironies."

"What is?"

"That sometimes the fellows with the least involvement are the ones who get the most involved. If this, for example, should come to the attention of some of the fellows higher up . . ."

"God forbid," Cockeye said, and again rolled his best eye.

"So let's just get the thing done, get the kid back, and hope this all blows over before Ganooch returns. That's the best we can hope for."

"I can have the bills for you by tomorrow at this time," Cockeye said.

"Good. Do you require a deposit?"

"Not from an old friend like you."

"What have you been working on lately?" Benny asked conversationally.

"Dollar bills," Cockeye said. "There's not much of a markup on them, but you do a bigger volume. Have you seen my recent work, Ben?"

"No, I haven't," Benny said. "As a matter of fact, I've never seen *any* of your work. But I'd certainly like to."

"I was running some bills off when you came in," Cockeye said. He walked to the printing press. "Let me show you," he said. "Then we can have our coffee."

He lifted a fresh dollar bill from the platen. "It's still a little wet," he said, "be careful." With the pride of creation gleaming in his best eye, he handed the bill to Benny. "Have a look," he said.

Benny looked at the bill. It seemed like very nice work. He blinked his eyes and looked at the bill again, more closely this time, and suddenly he did not feel like staying for coffee, suddenly he realized that getting Ganooch's kid back would be a lot more difficult than merely delivering fifty thousand dollars in counterfeit bills to those crazy maniacs who had taken the boy. Transfixed, he continued staring at the bill, his telephoto gaze zooming in on the picture of General George Washington:

"What do you think of it?" Cockeye asked, beaming.

"Well," Benny said, "it's a wee bit *off*, don't you think?"

"Really?" Cockeye said, and studied the bill. "Where do you think it's off?"

6: SNITCH

Nanny went to see Snitch Delatore early Thursday morning in the hope that he may have heard something about who had stolen little Lewis. The possibility that he had heard anything, since no one ever told him anything, was extremely remote, but Nanny was becoming somewhat desperate. A call from Benny Napkins the night before had apprised her of the difficulties he was having in raising the counterfeit money, an idea that had at first seemed eminently workable. Benny had told her he would get to work on another scheme he had, and that in the meantime she should let him know as soon as the kidnaper called her again. She did not know what Benny's other scheme was. She was, in fact, beginning to regret she'd contacted him at all.

She was also beginning to regret having contacted Snitch Delatore because conversation with him was proving somewhat difficult. She had been warned time and again never to tell Snitch anything unless she wished it to be re-channeled directly into the Police Department. She was determined not to tell him anything now. But at the same time, Snitch considered himself to be in the business of gathering information, and he was equally determined to get from Nanny whatever she had to offer. So they sat together in the sunshine on a bench in the United Nations Plaza Park, watching the traffic on the East River, and their discussion was, of necessity, a trifle circuitous.

"Tell me again why you came to see me," Snitch said.

"I wanted to know if you had heard anything," Nanny said.

"About what?" Snitch said.

"About anything."

"Well, I've heard a lot about a lot of things," Snitch said, which was an outright lie since he never heard anything about anything. "Which of those things was it you wanted to know about?"

"Well, I won't know what I want to know until I know what you know," Nanny said.

"Well," Snitch said, "if I don't know what you want to know, how can I know if what I know is what you want?"

Nanny looked out over the river to where a coal barge was sending up great puffs of smoke against the sky. She thought fleetingly of the Thames and of how simple and uncomplicated life had been in London, where she'd had a good position in Mayfair, not as pleasant perhaps as the one at Many Maples, but where a person certainly did not have to deal with types like Snitch.

"What I want to know about," she said at last, "is a crime."

"Which crime?" Snitch asked.

"Well, which crimes have you heard about?"

"Which crimes would you like to know about?"

"Whichever ones you've heard about."

"I've heard about a lot of them."

"Which ones?"

"Which ones would particularly interest you?"

"Any that you've heard about."

"Well, there are many crimes being perpetrated in this city," Snitch said, "and I'm privileged to know about almost each and every one of them. So if you have any specific crime in mind about which you are seeking information, all you need do is mention which crime it is, and I'll leaf through the catalogue of my mind and stop at the right card. Which crime is it that interests you?"

"Why don't you leaf through your catalogue aloud?" Nanny said. "When you come to the proper card, I'll ask you to stop."

"Nanny, you're a very nice lady," Snitch said, "but you're wasting my time. Unless we can come to some under . . ."

"Have you any information, for example, about a crime that may have been committed within the past few days?"

"Yesterday, do you mean?"

"Well, yesterday or the day before."

"By the day before yesterday, do you mean Tuesday?"

"Precisely."

"You're seeking information about a crime that was committed Tuesday?"

"Yes."

"Day or night?"

"Tuesday night."

"Very well," Snitch said, "now let's try to narrow that down, okay? Was this crime a big crime or a small crime?"

"A big crime."

"Was it bigger than a common misdemeanor?"

"Yes."

"Bigger than a Class-A misdemeanor?"

"Yes."

"Am I to take it that this crime was a felony?"

"Yes."

"Very well," Snitch said. "Now, as I'm sure you realize, there are felonies and there are felonies. Would this have been a big felony or a small felony?"

"A big one."

"By a big felony, do you mean a felony punishable by more than twenty years or by less than twenty years?"

"More. I think."

"In other words, we can be safe in eliminating felonies such as Assault, Forgery, and Grand Larceny, all of which by your definition would be considered *small* felonies."

"Yes."

"We are talking then about felonies such as Armed Robbery or Arson or Homicide or the like."

"Yes."

"Would the felony in question happen to be one of those I just mentioned?"

"No, it would not."

"May I intersperse a question at this point?" Snitch asked.

"Certainly."

"You have been with Mr. Ganucci for several years now. Why don't you seek his assistance in getting the information you need about this here crime in question?"

"Mr. Ganucci is in Italy."

"Cable him," Snitch said.

"I don't wish to interrupt his holiday."

"I'm sure he would be concerned in helping you get to the bottom of whatever . . ."

"I'm sure he would not be at all concerned," Nanny said flatly.

Snitch turned to study her face. His eyes narrowed. "Or is this something," he said slowly and evenly, "that might best not be brought to Mr. Ganucci's attention?"

"Like what?"

"Like a very large felony committed by one of his fellows, to which Mr. Ganucci is rightfully entitled to a certain share of the profits, and which was committed without neither his sanction nor his knowledge and which might piss him off considerably should he discover about it."

"No," Nanny said.

"Nothing like that?" Snitch said, clearly disappointed.

"No."

Snitch took off his hat and scratched his head. "You've got me stumped," he said.

"You've heard nothing?"

"Not about the kind of crime you have in question, if it's the kind of crime I think it is."

"I think you're thinking of the right kind of crime," Nanny said.

"I'll have to listen around some more," Snitch said.

"Then I take it we have nothing further to discuss," Nanny said.

"Not until I go on the earie again."

"Thank you," Nanny said, and rose from the bench. She smoothed her skirt, said, "Good day, Mr. Delatore," and walked off toward First Avenue.

Watching her as she departed, Snitch wondered what the hell they'd been talking about.

7: GARBUGLI

By eleven-thirty that morning, Snitch had all but forgotten his meeting with Nanny. There were more important matters on his mind. The more important matters were, in order: his former wife Roxanne (the little bitch); a man from Amarillo, Texas (who was now a Broadway Pokerino barker); and the alimony payments Roxanne kept demanding (even though she was currently living with the man from Texas, who rolled his own goddamn cigarettes).

"Is that fair?" Snitch wanted to know. "Mr. Garbugli? That I should have to keep paying her when she's sharing another man's bed and board?"

"It's not fair, but it's the law," Vito Garbugli said. He was a very busy man and would not have given Snitch the right time of day (no one did) had it not been for a call from a police lieutenant named Alexander Bozzaris, who had done a favor in the past and who now wanted a favor done (as he put it) "for one of the squad's trusted advisers." Garbugli had gone next door to his partner Azzecca's office and asked if he knew of anyone named Frank Delatore, and Azzecca had said, "That's probably Snitch

Delatore. Why?" Garbugli had then told him about the phone call from Bozzaris, and Azzecca had said, "Delatore's a rat. You should have said no." Whereupon Garbugli reminded his partner that a policy banker named Joe Dirigere had once donated seven thousand four hundred dollars to Bozzaris' favorite charity, for which the lieutenant had been willing to return to the fellows a full day's ribbons impounded in a raid, which work amounted to a lot of cold hard cash. Azzecca maintained that nobody had done anybody no favors, the transaction having been a simple act of commerce. But he allowed as how Snitch, though a rat, was not a particularly dangerous rat, so long as Garbugli told him nothing that could in any way be useful to the police. Garbugli shrugged and said, "He's only coming here to talk about his wife, Counselor."

Which Snitch had been doing for perhaps ten minutes now, complaining bitterly about her flagrant carryings-on with the Pokerino barker and continually asking, "Is it fair? Mr. Garbugli?"

"As long as she remains unmarried," Garbugli said, "she's entitled to the alimony payments awarded to her."

"But she's living with this big Texan," Snitch protested.

"It wouldn't matter if she was living with the Seven Dwarfs," Garbugli said. "You'd still have to pay her."

"I won't pay," Snitch said.

"In which case you'll go to jail. And while you're in jail, she'll continue her arrangement with this here Pokerino barker. You want my advice? Pay."

"It's not fair," Snitch said.

"My good friend," Garbugli said, "there is much on this road of life that is unfair, but we must all carry our share of the goddamn burden."

"Mr. Garbugli?" Snitch said.

"Yes?"

The telephone buzzed. "Excuse me," Garbugli said, and lifted the receiver. "Vito Garbugli speaking," he said. "What? Oh, certainly, I'll be right in, Mario." He rose swiftly and walked around his desk. "My partner. I'll just be a moment," he said, and went to the door separating his office from Azzecca's. The door closed behind him. Snitch sat in the leather armchair thinking about how unfair it was. He sat that way for perhaps five minutes. He was beginning to think Garbugli would not return; *that* wasn't fair either. The door to the outer office opened, and a long-legged, pretty redhead wearing a short beige skirt and a green blouse entered, walked quickly to Garbugli's desk, put a yellow sheet of paper on it, swiveled, smiled at Snitch, walked to the door again, and went out. The office was silent. Snitch got up and walked to the windows. On the street below, decent men like himself were going their merry way without having to worry about paying alimony to a bitch who was living with a big Texan who rolled his own cigarettes. Seven Dwarfs, some sense of humor the counselor had. Snitch glanced at the yellow sheet of paper the girl had put on Garbugli's desk. It looked very much like a telegram or something. Merely out of curiosity, Snitch began to read it:

western union   **Telegram**

```
CDU071 RWU809 CP084 14PD INTL FR CD CAPRI
18  2130
AZZGAR (AZZECCA & GARBUGLI)
    (145 WEST 45 ST) NYK
ESSENTIAL AND URGENT RAISE FIFTY DELIVERY SATURDAY
AUGUST 21 ADVISE
    CARMINE GANUCCI
```

WU 1201 (R 5-69)

Sure, Snitch thought, Ganooch sends telegrams all the way from Italy, and guys in the street go their merry way, while I have to pay alimony to somebody I hardly even met—I was only married to her, for Christ's sake, for sixteen lousy months! He sat in the leather chair again. At the window, the air conditioner hummed serenely. In a little while, he fell asleep.

When Garbugli came back into the office, he found his client snoring. He also found the cable from Carmine Ganucci. He quickly stuffed it into his pocket, shook Snitch by the shoulder, and asked him if there was anything else he wished to discuss. Snitch had difficulty coming awake and for one terrifying moment relived a time in Chicago when he had been shaken from sleep in the middle of a February night and asked why he had such a big mouth. He had answered, "*Who* has a big mouth?" and someone in the dark had said, "*You* have a big mouth," and Snitch had said, "Aw, come on, I do not." He established his surroundings now, assured Garbugli he had nothing more to ask (but that he wasn't ready to pay any alimony to no whore, neither), thanked the lawyer for his time, and left. At the desk outside, he bummed a cigarette from the redhead who had brought the cable in, and then went down to the street.

It was going to be a hot day.

He wondered if it was this hot in Italy. Probably not. He also wondered why it was ESSENTIAL AND URGENT that Carmine Ganucci RAISE FIFTY. Fifty *what*? Not measly dollars, that was for sure. Ganooch probably carried around ten times that amount just in case he had to tip a cabbie. Could it be fifty *thousand*? Was it essential and urgent that Ganooch raise fifty *thousand* by Saturday? That was a lot of money. People did not trip across fifty thousand dollars in the gutter every day. Nor did Ganooch's trusted governess come around every day asking about various and sundry felonies perpetrated on a Tuesday night.

Something was in the wind.

Snitch sensed this with the same rising excitement he had known in Chicago on February 14, 1929. He could barely refrain from dancing a little buck and wing right there on Forty-fifth Street. Something was in the wind, all right, something really big. And Snitch knew just the party who would love to hear all about it.

If he hadn't been temporarily broke, he'd have taken a taxi uptown.

In the office upstairs, Mario Azzecca and Vito Garbugli were conducting an intense examination. Or rather, Azzecca was conducting the examination; Garbugli mostly listened. Azzecca's witness was Marie Pupattola, the long-legged, redheaded secretary who had brought the cable into his partner's office and put it on his desk. Marie was a bit frightened by the intensity of Azzecca's questions. Also, she had just got her period yesterday.

"Was he asleep when you came in here?" Azzecca asked.

"Gee, I don't remember," Marie said.

"Try to remember!" he said. "Was he asleep in that chair when you brought the cable in?"

"Now, now, Counselor," Garbugli said.

"I don't remember," Marie said, knowing full well that Snitch had not been asleep because she had very definitely smiled at him, and she was not in the habit of smiling at people who were asleep.

"Were his eyes closed?"

"They could have been."

"Were they closed, or were they open?"

"Sometimes," Marie said, "when a person's eyes are closed, they could also look open."

"Did *his* look open or closed?"

"They looked closed," she said, which was a lie because they had looked very open, especially when she'd smiled at him.

"Then do you think he was asleep?"

"He could have been asleep," she said, "but gee, I don't remember."

"Do you think he saw this cable, Marie?"

"Gee, I don't know," Marie said. "Why would he have seen it?"

"Because you put it on the desk there, and he was right here in this room alone with it for Christ knows how many minutes."

"Now, now, Counselor," Garbugli said.

"*Would* he have looked at it?" Marie said. "I mean, if he was asleep?"

"*Was* he asleep?"

"He was very definitely asleep," she said.

"Are you sure?"

"I know a man when he's asleep or not, don't I?" she asked.

"Thank you, Marie," Garbugli said.

"Not at all," Marie said, and smiled at him the same way she had smiled at Snitch, and then went out to her desk.

"What do you think?" Garbugli said.

"I think she's a lying little twat, and that Snitch was awake with both eyes open, and that he read every word of that cable," Azzecca said.

"So do I," Garbugli said. "I think we had maybe better call Nonaka and ask him to look up our friend Snitch Delatore."

"Nonaka gives me the shivers," Azzecca said. "Besides, first things first. What do we do about this money Ganooch wants?"

"Send it," Garbugli said.

"Why do you suppose he needs that kind of money by Saturday?"

"I don't know," Garbugli said. "But if he cabled all the way from Capri, then it must be pretty . . ."

"*If* it was him who sent the cable," Azzecca said shrewdly.

"It's signed Carmine Ganucci, Counselor."

"That's not a signature," Azzecca said. "That's just a cable with the words 'Carmine Ganucci' on it. It could have been twelve different people who sent that cable. It could even be the *police* who sent that cable."

"The Naples police, do you mean?"

"Why not?"

"The Naples police can hardly write *Italian,* no less English."

"What I'm trying to say, Vito, is that perhaps this is a trap."

"What kind of trap?"

"I don't know. If I knew what kind of trap, I'd positively avoid it."

Garbugli shrugged. "Maybe Ganooch merely wishes to buy a little bauble for Stella."

"For *Stella*?" Azzecca said.

"Don't underestimate Stella," Garbugli said. "She has very lovely boobs."

"They're nice boobs, true," Azzecca said, "but they're not worth twenty-five thousand dollars apiece."

"I think we're safe in any respect," Garbugli said. "Let's say we send the cash, we're covered by his cable. We have the cable right here, requesting the money."

"But suppose he *didn't* send the cable?"

"We're still in the clear, Counselor."

"I think we should check it out first."

"We haven't got time. This is Thursday, and he wants the money by Saturday. If we send him a return cable, he first has to receive it. Then he has to cable back his okay. Then we have to raise the money . . ."

"There's more than that in petty cash alone. In the safety deposit box downtown."

"We'd have to clear it first with Paulie Secondo."

"We'd have to do that in any case."

"What do you suggest?"

"I suggest we cable Ganooch at the Quisisana to get his nod. If he *really* sent this cable, he'll tell us so. If he didn't send it, he'll want to know what the hell we're talking about."

"Let's compose the message, Counselor," Garbugli said.

Crosstown and uptown, Luther Patterson was about to compose a message of his own.

On the telephone yesterday, he had told the Ganucci governess (who had sounded like a very pleasant though bewildered lady indeed) that he would contact her at five o'clock this afternoon with instructions about the ransom money. Now, seated behind his typewriter at his desk in one corner of the book-lined living room, he inserted a blank sheet into the machine and began thinking. If there was one person he could count on at times like this, it was John Simon. If there was another person, it was Martin Levin. Between those two persons, a person didn't need any other persons. Luther Patterson believed this with all his heart. When he found himself in a prosodic jam, either or both of them was (*were*, John?) ready to stand up and be counted.

Luther looked at the digital clock on his desk. He was delighted that the Japanese had begun manufacturing digital clocks in such astonishing volume because, to tell the truth, he had never been very good at telling time. He attributed this to the fact that his sister had been such a whiz at it. When they were both kids together, he would sometimes deliberately confuse the hour with the minute hand out of pure spite, reporting the time as a quarter to five, for example, when it was really twenty-five past nine (ha!) hoping to mix up his smart-ass little brat of a sister, who never *did* get mixed up and who would announce the correct time each time from the face of her Mickey Mouse watch. He no longer hated his sister. Neither could he tell time too well. Which was why he was grateful for the digital clock, and the clear bold numbers that read . . .

Luther put on his eyeglasses because he couldn't see too well, either.

The time was . . .

1:56.

"John," he said aloud, "Martin—we've got some important writing to do here."

He did not yet know how he would deliver his note once he had composed it. He supposed that the Ganucci estate would be swarming with policemen by this time, even though the governess had assured him she had not told them of the kidnaping. He found this difficult to believe, and yet there had been no newspaper stories about it, no radio or television reports. It was his guess that he had actually succeeded in scaring the retired soft drinks magnate witless; Ganucci had undoubtedly requested complete silence until the boy was safely returned.

He wondered why the governess had told him Ganucci was in Italy. Had that been the truth, or merely a stall? It didn't matter, either way. Luther knew without question that if he'd had a son of his own, and if that son had been kidnaped, he'd have returned home immediately from wherever he happened to be vacationing—Montauk Point, Block Island, places even more distant, *anywhere*. So he was fairly confident that, even if Ganucci *had* been abroad, he was undoubtedly home by now, scurrying around to sell securities and raise the cash he needed to ransom the boy. The thought of all that frantic activity on the part of the retired millionaire amused Luther. But it was tinged with a touch of sadness as well. He had been married to Ida for fourteen years now; they had been childless all that time, except for a Pekingese dog they'd had in 1969. Ida doted on the Ganucci boy now as if he were her very own, leaving a night light on for him last night, making blueberry pancakes for him this morning (Luther had found the pancakes inedible, but the boy had eaten them ravenously), and constantly carrying snacks and milk to the back bedroom in which he was locked. Their inability to produce children called to mind one of Luther's favorite John Simon passages. He went to the *Collected Works* now, took the volume from the shelf, opened it to a page finger-smudged through constant reference, and silently read it over again:

A story or poem, unable to bask in length, must operate in depth, height, thickness. It must set up inner relationships, echoes, implications, suggestions; utilize the space between the lines; curl up on itself to achieve pregnancy.

Luther brushed a tear from his cheek.

There was work to be done. The first draft of any literary endeavor was always the most difficult, for it was this draft that embodied the initial creative thrust. John Simon undoubtedly knew and understood that basic tenet. Inspired by what he had just read, knowing he could never equal its power but determined to try nonetheless, Luther replaced the scrapbook on its shelf, sat down at the typewriter again and, unable to bask in length, was beginning to create his second ransom note when a brilliant idea struck him. He rushed to the bookcase again, gathered both Simon *and* Levin into his arms and, clutching them gratefully to his chest, rushed to his desk, his scissors, and his pastepot.

*   *   *

If there was anything more difficult than composing a cable to Italy at twenty-six and a half cents a word, neither Azzecca nor Garbugli could imagine what. Just the address alone took up five words.

"How many words is that?" Garbugli asked Azzecca, who had wheeled over the typing cart and who was sitting behind the machine with his hands resting on the keys.

"Five," Azzecca said.

"Twenty-six and a half cents a word, that's highway robbery," Garbugli said.

"We better keep it very short," Azzecca warned. "If Ganooch really *did* send that cable, he's not going to like us squandering money to *confirm* that he sent it."

"Right, Counselor," Garbugli said.

"How does this sound?" Azzecca said. "DID YOU SEND A CABLE? AZZECCA-GARBUGLI."

"That's a little impersonal, isn't it?"

"Yes, but it's brief."

"Also, Counselor, it don't indicate that *we* received a cable. Ganooch may have sent a cable to his sister, for example, in which case he would reply CERTAINLY I SENT A CABLE, and we still wouldn't know whether it was this *here* cable he sent."

"I see what you mean," Azzecca said. "How about DID YOU SEND THIS HERE CABLE WE RECEIVED?"

"How about just DID YOU SEND US THIS HERE CABLE?"

"That's shorter," Azzecca agreed, "but how about IS THIS HERE CABLE YOURS? That's even shorter."

"Yes, but it don't necessarily mean that this here cable is this here cable *here*."

"Hold it a minute," Azzecca said. "I think I've got it." He

began typing. Garbugli opened his jacket and allowed the sun-shine to strike the Phi Beta Kappa key he had earned at City College. Once, in this very office, Carmine Ganucci had said to him, "What the hell is *that* thing?" and he had proudly an-swered, "Why, that's my Phi Bete key, Ganooch."

"Yeah?" Ganooch had said.

"Why, yes."

"What does he mean?" Ganooch asked Azzecca.

"Phi Beta Kappa."

"Yeah, what's that?"

"An honor society."

"Italian?" Ganooch had asked.

That had been a long time ago, of course, long before Nanny had begun bringing culture to the big old house in Larchmont. Ganooch now knew what a Phi Beta Kappa key was. He had only recently, in fact, asked Garbugli where he'd stolen it, as he admired it greatly and desired one of his own. His fingers laced across his expansive middle, Garbugli looked down at the key now and luxuriated in the afternoon sunshine that streamed through the window. Azzecca typed furiously and swiftly for perhaps thirty seconds, stopped abruptly, shouted, "There!" and pulled the sheet from the machine.

"Let's see it, Counselor," Garbugli said, and his partner handed him the typewritten sheet:


```
CARMINE GANUCCI
QUISISANA
CAPRI, ITALY

IS OUR CABLE YOURS?

AZZECCAGARBUGLI.
```

"I put our names together like one name," Azzecca said. "Save twenty-six and a half cents that way." He paused. Garbugli was studying the message intently. "What do you think?" Azzecca asked.

"I think we should call him on the telephone," Garbugli answered.

8: BOZZARIS

Alexander Bozzaris was not a crook. He was a cop. In his mind, there was a big difference. Only once in his lifetime had he suffered through an identity crisis, and that was when he tried to rape his wife. He had just for the fun of it dressed up as a bum one night, sneaked into his own house (he had to smile just thinking of it), and tried to violate his own wife. He was arrested for this, and held for three hours in a Bronx precinct even though he had shown all the detectives his badge and warned that he would bring them up on charges unless they released him immediately. His wife, however, insisted to the detectives that she had never before seen him in her life, and that he had broken into her bedroom shouting "Rape!" and so it was the word of a nice Jewish lady against that of an obvious Greek pervert. Bozzaris was not released until Captain O'Rourke, who ran the precinct, came up himself and verified that Bozzaris was a cop.

He was reaching for a ringing telephone on his desk when Snitch walked into his office that afternoon. "Hello, Snitch," he said, and motioned him to a straight-backed chair across the room, and lifted the receiver from its cradle.

"Bozzaris here," he said into the mouthpiece. "Just a second, let me get a piece of paper." He opened the top drawer of his desk, pulled out a blank sheet of Police Department stationery, pinned it to the desk with his elbow, picked up a pencil, and said, "Shoot!" into the mouthpiece. Across the room, Snitch crossed his legs, and then uncrossed them again. He had had to go to the bathroom ever since he'd stumbled across his priceless information. He resented the telephone intrusion now because he was very anxious to begin bargaining with Bozzaris. Impatiently, he listened as Bozzaris spoke into the phone.

"Right," Bozzaris said. "Where? Oh, I see, our man downtown at Western Union. What? Well, be that as it may, what does the cable read? Just a minute, let me write this down. Addressed to *who*? Right, right, I've got it. Go ahead."

Snitch uncrossed his legs again.

"Right," Bozzaris said. "From Capri, right. What's the message?"

Snitch crossed his legs.

"Essential and urgent," Bozzaris said, "raise fifty delivery Saturday August 21. Advise."

Snitch opened his mouth, uncrossed his legs, and leaned forward in his chair.

"What's the signature?" Bozzaris asked.

"Carmine Ganucci," Snitch said glumly.

"What?" Bozzaris said.

"Nothing," Snitch said, and started out of the office.

"Just a minute there!" Bozzaris yelled. Into the mouthpiece, he said, "I'll call you back later." He hung up, rose from his desk, and intercepted Snitch in the squadroom outside, where Bozzaris' various fellows were busy at work typing up Detective Division reports. The squadroom had about it the air of a soggy, used, cardboard coffee container. It had been painted Institutional Apple Green circa 1919, and had since been repainted some two dozen times, always the same apple green, a color peculiarly vulnerable to grime. It was reasonable to estimate that there were more fingerprints on those dingy squadroom walls than there were in the filing cabinets lining them. Some of the cabinets were made of wood; the remainder were metal, painted a dark green for decorative contrast. Similarly, the detectives' desks were a chic combination of scarred wood and battered metal. A matching metal detention cage for obstreperous prisoners dominated one corner of the room. A bulletin board with various departmental flyers (including an announcement for the Annual Departmental Golf Meet) was on the wall adjacent to the lieutenant's office. It was alongside this bulletin board that Bozzaris grabbed Snitch by the elbow and said, "What's your hurry, Snitch?"

"Well," Snitch said, "I see that you're busy and all, so there's no sense hanging around."

"Never too busy for you, Snitch," Bozzaris said, and grinned. "What was it you wished to see me about?"

His expansive welcome was not at all feigned. Detective Lieutenant Alexander Bozzaris considered Snitch a very good adviser, one of the best the department had. His admiration was based on the fact that Snitch had delivered an excellent tip to the Chicago police back in 1929, on St. Valentine's Day to be exact. Snitch had told the minions of the law that a little get-together was being planned for a garage on North Wells Street. The only thing that had been wrong about Snitch's information was the address; the blowout was being held on North Clark. But everyone makes mistakes from time to time. The fellows in Chicago, willing to forgive Snitch for *both* his errors, quickly promoted a quiet beer party, the proceeds of which went to pay Snitch's hospital expenses and to buy him a fine set of crutches besides. Shortly thereafter, Snitch decided to move to New York.

The fellows in New York had heard of Snitch's near coup, and decided there was no sense repeating anything to him because then there would be all the trouble afterwards of transporting him out to some Godforsaken potato patch on Long Island. At first, the fellows talked to him about nothing but the weather. Later, they rarely said anything at *all* to him. Eventually, as folklore became myth, Snitch came to be considered a very dull conversationalist, all the more reason to avoid discussion with him. These days, the only people who talked to Snitch were the police, who were still filled with admiration for his Chicago derring-do, who still offered him money for information, and who sometimes squared raps for him—which raps were generally bum raps invented by the police themselves to keep Snitch forever in their debt so that he would continue to pass on valuable underworld secrets nobody in his right mind ever told him.

"What have you heard?" Bozzaris asked.

"Plenty," Snitch said, figuring all was not lost, despite the fact that Bozzaris was already privy to information about Ganooch's cable.

"Come into my office and we'll have some coffee," Bozzaris said. "Sam!" he yelled to one of his fellows. "Two cups of coffee on the double!"

"We are out of coffee, Skipper!" Sam yelled back.

"Be that as it may," Bozzaris answered, and led Snitch into his office. "Please sit down," he said, and beckoned to an easy chair usually reserved for the Police Commissioner, the District Attorney, and various other municipal dignitaries who never visited Bozzaris' office. Snitch accepted the seat with all the dignity of President Richard Milhous Nixon accepting a hard hat from construction workers.

"How did you know who signed that cable?" Bozzaris asked, getting directly to the point.

"I have ways and means," Snitch answered.

"For what purpose does Carmine Ganucci need this money?" Bozzaris asked.

"There was a major felony committed on Tuesday night," Snitch answered.

"Be that as it may," Bozzaris said, "I don't see the connection."

"Are you familiar with the lady who lives at Many Maples?" Snitch asked.

"Are you referring to Stella Ganucci?"

"No," Snitch said.

"Stella Ganucci has a very spectacular set of jugs," Bozzaris said wistfully.

"True, but I mean the lady who lives there and takes care of the Ganucci boy."

"I remember seeing Stella Ganucci perform in Union City when I was a mere boy myself," Bozzaris said, "and when her name at the time was Stella Stardust. She had a little light on the end of each tit, and it shone in the dark, both of them."

"Yes, but I mean the lady known as Nanny."

"I don't believe I've had the pleasure."

"Nanny came to me this morning to ask about a major felony committed on Tuesday night."

"What did you tell her?"

"Nothing. But I'll bet you all the money in China that Ganooch's request for fifty grand is linked to that felony."

"Which felony would that be?" Bozzaris asked.

"I don't know yet," Snitch replied. "But it's something big, I'm sure of that."

"Mmm," Bozzaris said, and laced his fingers across his chest. He thought for a moment, cleared his throat, leaned forward in the swivel chair, put both elbows on the desk, fingers still laced, and said, "As I'm sure you know, Snitch, I'm considered a fighter in the department, witness my name. I was a fighter even back when I was a patrolman walking a beat on Staten Island, and I've continued to be a fighter over all the years that have brought me to my present fame and position. If there's one thing I can't abide, it's evil. Evil to me is the opposite of good. It's the death force, as contrary to the life force. Have you ever noticed, Snitch, that 'evil' spelled backwards is 'live'?"

"No, I never noticed that," Snitch said.

"Try it," Bozzaris said.

"How do you spell 'evil'?" Snitch asked.

"E-v-i-l, which is l-i-v-e spelled backwards."

"Yes, that's right, now that you mention it," Snitch said.

"And if there's one thing I hate worse than evil, it's *organized* evil. Carmine Ganucci and his fellows represent organized evil to me. Snitch, I'm going to tell you something in all honesty. I've always been a rebel, witness my name. I do not consider it fair that Carmine Ganucci and his fellows, through their organized evil, are reaping huge profits while my salary as a detective lieutenant in charge of a crack squad is a mere $19,781.80 a year. Do you think that's fair, Snitch?"

"I don't think it's fair, Lieutenant," Snitch said. "On the other hand, there is much on this road of life that is unfair, but we must all carry our share of the goddamn burden."

"Snitch?" Bozzaris said.

"Yes, Lieutenant?"

"Snitch, I do not like profanity."

"Forgive me," Snitch said.

"Profanity and evil go hand in hand."

"I, myself, rarely swear," Snitch said.

"Be that as it may," Bozzaris said. "Do you understand what I'm trying to tell you?"

"I don't think so," Snitch said.

"Why do you think that fellow at Western Union called *me*?" Bozzaris said.

"To tell you about the cable Ganooch sent."

"Yes, but why *me*? He's a trusted adviser, Snitch, same as you, though hardly as well known or respected. Now why do you think he called *me* instead of someone on the D.A.'s Special Squad?"

"Why?" Snitch said.

"Because he knows I have vowed unending warfare against the forces of evil," Bozzaris said.

"Oh," Snitch said.

"Carmine Ganucci is evil. So when this fellow at Western Union gets hold of a message from Ganucci to his lawyers, he calls *me*, knowing full well I'll *do* something about it, whereas those fellows on the D.A.'s squad would sit around on their asses all week without making a move, though I dislike profanity."

"I see," Snitch said.

"Also, he knew I would pay him twenty-five dollars for the information," Bozzaris said. "The same way I always pay you twenty-five dollars for any information you come up with."

"Well, could I have the twenty-five now?" Snitch asked. "I'm a little short of cash these days."

"I'd be happy to give you twenty-five dollars this very minute," Bozzaris said. "The trouble is you haven't come up with any information I didn't already possess."

"I have so," Snitch said.

"As for example?"

"Well, you didn't know about the big felony committed on Tuesday night, for example, did you?" Snitch said.

"I know about four hundred and ten felonies committed in this very precinct alone," Bozzaris said.

"But you didn't know this *particular* felony might be connected to . . ."

"*Which* felony?" Bozzaris said, and smiled. "Do you see what I mean, Snitch? So far, no new information."

"Well, what is it you'd like to know?" Snitch asked. "*Which* felony it was?"

"I'm not interested in felonies," Bozzaris said. "Felonies are a dime a dozen around here. I think I can say with some measure of pride that there are more felonies committed in this precinct than in any other precinct in the entire city. So don't tell me about felonies. I'm not interested in felonies."

"Well," Snitch said, "what *are* you interested in?"

"The fruits of organized evil," Bozzaris said. "Money. I am primarily interested in intercepting that fifty thousand dollars *before* it gets to Naples."

"If I may say so, Lieutenant," Snitch said, "I don't know very much about organized evil, of course, but I'm willing to bet those fellows send a *check* to Naples."

"I beg to differ with you," Bozzaris said, "and I'll make allowances for your ignorance since *I've* made a lifelong study of organized evil, whereas you have not. But it's been my experience that these fellows *never* write checks. *Never.* You can mark that down as a cardinal rule."

"Well, maybe so," Snitch said, "in which case it would be a simple matter to arrange a transfer of funds from a New York bank to a Naples bank. If there's one thing I know about organized evil, and I admit I don't know very much, it's that these fellows are very well organized."

"Be that as it may," Bozzaris said, "not too many of them are willing to risk keeping records that show large amounts of money being transferred from one country to another, nor even from one city *block* to another. That's one sure way of getting the Internal Revenue Service down on their asses,

Snitch, witness what happened to Al Capone, and pardon the French."

Snitch lowered his head in respect.

"Cash," Bozzaris said. "That's the secret of organized evil. Cash on the barrelhead. Do you want to know what I think?"

"What?" Snitch said.

"I think somebody's going to raise fifty thousand bucks in cold hard cash, after which a trusted messenger will get on an airplane, fly to Naples, and put it right in Carmine Ganucci's hands. *That's* what I think."

"Well, maybe," Snitch said.

"If you can find out when and where that money will be raised and/or delivered to the man who will carry it to Italy, *that* might be worth twenty-five dollars to the hardworking fellows of this squad, who as you may know pay for information out of their own pockets."

"I didn't know that."

"It's a little-known fact," Bozzaris said, "but true. And if you can deliver this information, we might also forget the other little charge against you that's still on the books."

"What charge?" Snitch asked, going pale.

It was eight P.M. in Italy when Carmine Ganucci was called to the telephone at Faraglioni, where he was having dinner with Stella and a retired rhinoplastician from Jersey City. He was annoyed at being called to the phone just when the *gamberoni* were being served, and even more annoyed after he identified himself and heard Vito Garbugli's voice on the other end of the line.

"What is it, Vito?" he asked.

"Did you send a cable?" Garbugli said.

"Yes."

"To us?"

"Of course to you."

"Is it true what you said in the cable?"

"Every word."

"How do you wish delivery made?"

"By trusted messenger," Ganucci said.

"When?"

"Put him on a plane to Rome tomorrow night."

"I thought you wanted this in Naples."

"There's no flights from New York to Naples," Ganucci said. "He has to transfer in Rome. Make sure you tell him to transfer in Rome."

"I'll tell him."

"You always have to tell these dopes, or they forget to transfer."

"I'll tell him, don't worry," Garbugli said.

"And let me know what time he'll arrive. I'll arrange for someone to meet him Saturday."

"Right, I'll call you back later and let you know exactly . . ."

"Send a night letter," Ganucci said.

"Right, a night letter."

"How's little Lewis?"

"I don't know. Do you want me to call the house and find out?"

"No, it's twenty-five cents to Larchmont. Has Nanny been getting my postcards?"

"I don't know. If you want me to call . . ."

"I been writing almost every day," Ganucci said. "Airmail. It cost a hundred fifteen lira to send a postcard airmail. What else do you have to say to me?"

"Nothing."

"Then hang up, this is costing a fortune," Ganucci said, and hung up.

* * *

At the Twenty-third Street and Lexington Avenue branch of the First National City Bank, at 2:37 P.M., New York time, Benny Napkins was withdrawing from his savings account all but $216.00, which he thought he had better keep for a rainy day in case The Jackass goofed tonight. He did not see how The Jackass could possibly muff the play, but Benny was well aware that people sometimes make mistakes, and he figured he might just as well have enough to cover the plane fare to Honolulu in case something went wrong. *The best laid schemes o' mice an men gang aft a-gley,* he quoted silently, and then said to the cashier, "I want four thousand in hundred-dollar bills, and two thousand in singles."

"Two thousand in *singles*?" the cashier said.

"That's correct," Benny said.

The cashier began counting.

Benny knew that his plan was slightly dishonest, but on the other hand he had not asked some crazy maniac to steal Ganooch's son, nor had he asked Nanny to call him for assistance. He was handling the entire matter professionally and coolly, he thought. At ten o'clock tonight, if all went according to plan, and if The Jackass did not goof, Benny would be in possession of the ransom money and perhaps a little bit more for his troubles. Provided Celia Mescolata had arranged for the game; he would not know about that until five-thirty. In the meantime, he picked up the stack of bills—two thousand singles and forty hundreds—asked the cashier for a rubber band, rolled the bills into an enormous wad, century notes showing, snapped the rubber band around the roll, thanked the cashier, and left the bank.

He wondered if he should call The Jackass again, just to make sure he understood the plan. The Jackass was not too bright. The Jackass sometimes had trouble remembering his own telephone number. Still, it was best not to pressure a man once he had agreed to an action. There was no sense overtraining a good horse or a good fighter. The Jackass understood very few things in life, but one thing he understood fine was larceny.

Benny walked up Lexington Avenue to his apartment. He was very nervous, so he decided to ask Jeanette Kay if she was in the mood. Jeanette Kay said she might be, so long as they were finished by four o'clock, at which time *Dark Shadows* came on.

Nanny looked at the picture on the front of the card and thought it highly attractive. She turned the card over and read it:

Nanny read the card again, and then another time. He had mentioned nothing about coming home, and that was good. According to the itinerary he had left on the desk in his study, he and Stella would not be leaving Italy until Sunday, August 29. Apparently nothing had yet happened to change those plans—although Nanny was quite aware of the fact that it took five or six days for his postcards to get here, and that he might just pop in the front door without any forewarning. Should something like that happen, should the Ganuccis suddenly decide to leave Italy, or (oh my God!) already *be* in transit from Italy, and unexpectedly walk into the house trailing baggage and asking for little Lewis . . .

The thought was terrifying.

Nanny decided to call Benny Napkins again. She went into the study, slid the doors shut behind her even though the house was quite empty and still, went to the desk near the leaded casement windows now spilling afternoon sunshine into the room, and dialed Benny's number in Manhattan. He took an inordinately long time to answer the phone, and then he said, rather gruffly, she thought, "Who the hell is this?"

"This is Nanny."

"Oh," he said. "Oh, hello, Nanny. Listen, Nanny, can you call back in a little while? Like in about ten minutes? What?" he said, and Nanny got the distinct impression he had turned away from the phone for a moment. His voice came back again, a trifle louder. "Make that *fifteen* minutes, okay?" he said.

"I'm very worried," Nanny said.

"Yes, I can understand, but everything's under control," Benny said, "and there's nothing to worry about. Nanny, could you maybe call back in about ten, fifteen minutes, and we'll go over the whole thing then, okay?"

"I want to discuss it now," Nanny said.

There was a long silence on the line. Then Benny said, wearily, she thought, "What is it, Nanny?"

"What progress have you made?" Nanny asked.

"I have arranged a poker game for this evening. Or at least, I have spoken to a friend of mine about arranging one. She'll be calling me later to let me know whether or not the game is on. Nanny, I've got a good idea. Why don't you call me back at say five-thirty, six o'clock? By then I should know whether we got a game or not, and I can . . ."

"A poker game, did you say?"

"Yes, that's right."

"How can you think of playing cards at a time like this?" Nanny asked.

"I hope to take fifty thousand dollars out of that game, if all goes well," Benny said. "Nanny, this is not something we can discuss over the telephone, as you never know who's listening these days."

"Will you let me know later about the game?"

"Very definitely. Have you heard from those crazy maniacs yet?"

"Not yet. They said five o'clock."

"All right then, I'll call you back around six or so, and we can exchange information at that time. Does that sound all right to you, Nanny?"

"Yes, that sounds fine," Nanny said.

"Good," he said, abruptly she thought, and hung up.

9: AZZECCA

When the telephone rang at five-fifteen, Nanny was certain the kidnaper was calling at last with the instructions he had promised. Her delicate hand trembling, she lifted the receiver.

"Hello?" she said.

"Nanny? This is Benny Napkins. Everything's set for tonight. I'll call you as soon as the game is over. I hope to have the money by then."

"Good," Nanny said.

"Have you heard from the kidnaper yet?"

"No."

"He didn't call?"

"No."

"Did you look in the mailbox? Maybe he left the instructions there."

"Nobody could be that stupid," Nanny said.

"I would put nothing past this crazy maniac," Benny said. "Go check the mailbox and call me back."

"All right," she said, and hung up.

The second note, as Benny had surmised, was waiting in

the mailbox. Like the first note, it was fashioned of newspaper and magazine print clipped out and pasted to a sheet of blank white typing paper. Nanny had no way of knowing, of course, that the kidnaper had painstakingly scissored the words from reviews written by his two favorite critics. In the half-light of dusk, she stood by the mailbox and read the note out loud, the words echoing and floating away up the long driveway to Many Maples, airborne, inspired:

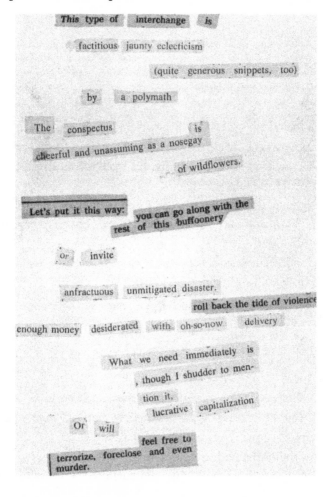

She went into the house and called Benny Napkins at once.

"I have another note from him," she said.

"What does it say?" Benny asked.

"I don't *know*," Nanny answered.

At seven o'clock that evening, one of Bozzaris' detectives picked up a man who looked suspicious for several reasons. One reason he looked suspicious was that he was a stranger to the precinct. Another reason was that he was straddling another man and pummeling him with both fists in the middle of the sidewalk outside a cafeteria not two blocks from the station house. He kept telling the detective who picked him up that he had only been acting in self-defense, but the detective knew a murderous stranger when he saw one. He brought the man up to the squadroom, whereupon it was promptly discovered that he was carrying on his person $10,000 in cash.

The man's name was William Shakespeare.

"Do you expect me to believe that?" Bozzaris asked.

"That's my name," the man answered in perfect English, which was suspicious in itself.

"Where do you live, Willie?"

"Downtown. On Mott Street."

"Why?"

"I like Chinese girls."

"Be that as it may," Bozzaris said, "what were you doing up here in the confines of my precinct, aside from committing assault on that poor man who was taken to the hospital?"

"That poor man tried to hold me up," Willie said. "I was protecting my life's savings from him."

"There are rarely daylight holdups in this precinct," Bozzaris said.

"Well, there was almost one today," Willie said. "Until I foiled it."

"One theory of criminal investigation," Bozzaris said, "is that the person who invites a criminal act is as guilty as the perpetrator of that act. That is an old Hebraic theory, if you are familiar with rabbinical law."

"I am not," Willie said.

"Be that as it may. A person who carries around ten thousand dollars in cash could be considered provocative, wouldn't you agree?"

"I needed the money," Willie said. "Which is why I came up here to draw it out of my savings account."

"For what purpose did you need the money?" Bozarris asked.

"For a personal purpose."

"Such as?"

A knock sounded discreetly on the lieutenant's door. "Enter," Bozzaris said, and a detective walked in and put a sheet of paper on the desk. "Thank you, Sam," Bozzaris said, and picked up the sheet of paper. "What do you do for a living, Willie?" Bozzaris asked.

"I manufacture mah-jong tiles. I became interested in the game and also in Chinese girls when I was a resident of Hong Kong many years ago."

"Willie," Bozzaris said, looking up, "according to this sheet of paper here, you are a known gambler in the Fifth and also the Ninth Precinct. What do you have to say about that?"

"I sometimes play cards, yes."

"You have also sometimes been arrested for Bookmaking, and Keeping a Gaming and Betting Establishment, and also Cheating at Gambling."

"Yes, sometimes," Willie admitted.

"*Many* times, it says here, and for the same offense a few times, in fact. An Assault charge added to this illustrious record might prove very troublesome," Bozzaris said, "in terms of the amount of time you might have to spend incarcerated."

"That man was attempting to hold me up," Willie said. "He probably saw my roll when I was paying my check in the cafeteria, and decided to follow me. It's no crime to protect yourself."

"Be that as it may," Bozzaris said. "It's also no crime for the District Attorney's office to automatically assume that a known gambler with a previous and lengthy record might be at fault in an Assault case where the arresting officer had to pull him off a man lying flat on his back on the sidewalk. The penalty for Assault in the Second Degree, which is probably what the charge would be, is five years. That's even if you did *not* have a previous record. I see here that you are a three-time loser, Willie, and I do not have to tell you what a fourth felony conviction could mean in terms of interminable incarceration."

"This is ridiculous," Willie said. "The man really *was* trying to steal my goddamn money!"

"Why were you carrying around so much money to begin with?"

"My sister needs it."

"For what?"

"My sister, whose name is Mary Shakespeare, and who lives on . . ."

"We are not interested in your family geniality here," Bozzaris said.

"My sister is going out to San Francisco to organize a protest there."

"Against what?"

"Conditions," Willie said, "which as you know are bad all over. It costs a lot of money to organize a protest, and I agreed to lend her my meager life's savings."

"That is pure and simple bullshit," Bozzaris said. "Pardon the French."

"It is the God's honest truth."

"Be that as it may, why did you *really* withdraw ten thousand dollars from your bank?"

"It has nothing whatsoever to do with the card game," Willie said.

"What card game?" Bozzaris asked.

"Do we forget all about the possible Assault charge, which is a bum rap anyway since I was the victim of an intended holdup?"

"I am not in a position to make promises of any nature," Bozzaris said.

"In that case, I am not in a position to reveal anything about the card game."

"What card game?" Bozzaris asked.

"What card game?" Willie answered.

"The card game which," Bozzaris said, "if your information about it is valuable to me, which I doubt that it will be, I might be willing to forget that you were pounding a man into the sidewalk, provided the man doesn't drop dead in the hospital, in which case we will have, of course, a homicide on our hands."

"Do I walk out of here meanwhile?" Willie asked.

"Tell me about the card game," Bozzaris said.

"What would you like to know?"

"When?"

"Tonight. Eight o'clock sharp."

"Where?"

"Celia Mescolata's."

"Blackjack?"

"Poker."

"The stakes?"

"Very high."

"How many players?"

"Six."

"Mmmm," Bozzaris said.

Somewhere on Capri, there was music.

They had taken an after-dinner stroll along the Via Quisisana, and then had stopped for a *granita* in the Piazzetta. Now, with the windows of their bedroom open to the soft night air, Stella tried to sleep while somewhere someone strummed a guitar and sang, she supposed, of unrequited love. It did not help that Carmine was snoring.

"Carmine?" she said.

"Mrmh."

"Are you asleep?"

"Yes."

"Carmine?"

"Mrmh."

"I want to talk to you."

"I'm asleep, I told you."

"Carmine, I have a feeling that something terrible has happened to Lewis."

"Nothing has happened to Lewis, go to sleep."

"How do you know nothing has happened to him?"

"Nanny knows exactly where we are. If anything was wrong, she'd call. That's how I know."

"Still."

"Go to sleep, Stella."

"All right, Carmine. Good night, Carmine."

"Good night, Stella."

Stella listened to the guitar. She wished she understood Italian. Thirty years ago, when Carmine asked her to marry him, she had answered, "But I don't understand Italian, Carmine."

"What's that got to do with love?" he said.

"Suppose we were out with some of your friends, and they began talking Italian?"

"I would tell them to talk English," Carmine said.

"Yes, but would they do it?"

"They would do it," he said, and gave a short emphatic nod that convinced her immediately. Carmine, who had been twenty years her senior even then, was true to his word. Whenever any of his friends began talking Italian in her presence, he would say, "Talk English." As a result, Stella *still* didn't understand Italian. Not that she minded, except on a night like this when she was so homesick, and a guitar player was singing songs she couldn't translate.

"Carmine?" she said.

"Mrmh."

"Carmine, I'm homesick."

"We'll be going home at the end of the month, go to sleep."

"Carmine, aren't you homesick?"

"No."

"Don't you miss Lewis?"

"Yes, but I'm not homesick."

"Don't you miss the house?"

"Only the darkroom," he said. "Go to sleep."

Mario Azzecca lived on Sutton Place South in an apartment building that had two doormen. The doormen were there so that none of the tenants would be burglarized in their sleep or mugged in the elevator. A third man ran the elevator, which meant that the bastions were well guarded against criminal assault at every hour of the day or night. Paulie Secondo, carrying fifty thousand dollars in cash and a round-trip airline ticket to Naples-via-Rome, arrived at Azzecca's building at twenty minutes past eight. He was announced by the doorman and promptly asked to go right up, sir, elevator on the left, seventh floor, apartment 7G as in George.

Mario Azzecca was sitting in his living room waiting for the Delacorte fountain to go on. It went on every night at eight-thirty sharp, shooting a spray of water some hundred feet into the air, and was not turned off again until ten. From Azzecca's living room, he could see clear across the East River to the southerly tip of Welfare Island, where Delacorte had erected the fountain for an estimated cost of three hundred thousand dollars. It was rumored that the fountain cost twenty-five thousand dollars a year to operate, and that it had been constructed for the amusement and amazement of United Nations delegates, but Mario Azzecca firmly believed it had been placed there for his pleasure alone. For hours on end, he would watch the display with unflagging interest. It was even better than watching the traffic on the Queensboro Bridge, which was also fascinating. He was, in truth, a trifle annoyed that Paulie Secondo arrived just a few minutes before the fountain was scheduled to erupt against the nighttime sky.

"Have you got the money?" he asked, somewhat brusquely.

"I have got the money," Paulie said. Paulie spoke with a distinct Italian accent that was sometimes embarrassing. Being Italian himself, Azzecca did not mind dealing with other Italians, but he drew the line at outright greaseballs—unless they happened to be very high up in the organization, which Paulie Secondo happened to be. Reflecting on the hierarchy (while nonetheless keeping one eye on the southern exposure), Azzecca decided it might be judicious to adopt a more cheerful manner.

"I'm sorry we had to put you through all this trouble, Paulie," he said. "But Ganooch needs the money right away."

"No trouble," Paulie said. "He told you why?"

"No."

Paulie shrugged. "No matter. He wants the money, he gets the money."

"There it goes," Azzecca said, and looked at his watch.

"What?" Paulie said.

"The fountain."

"Oh," Paulie said, and peered through the window. "Nice," he said, and turned away without interest. He reached into his jacket pocket and threw a bulging envelope onto the glass-topped coffee table. "Fifty thousand," he said. "In hundred-dollar bills, okay?"

"Fine," Azzecca said.

Paulie threw an airlines folder onto the table beside the envelope. "One ticket New York-Rome, Rome-Naples," he said. "And return."

"What airline?" Azzecca asked.

Paulie raised his eyebrows. "What airline you think?" he said.

"Who do you want us to send?" Azzecca asked.

"It's done," Paulie said.

"What do you mean?"

"On the ticket. It was necessary to give a name."

"Who?"

"Someone of little importance. Something goes wrong, we want no connection, *capisce*?"

"Yes, of course."

"Get the ticket and the money to him, tell him to be on the Alitalia plane tomorrow night at ten o'clock. He will be met in Naples on Saturday at two." Paulie looked through the window again. "How long does that thing shoot water?" he asked.

"Until ten."

"Looks like somebody laying on his back and taking a piss in the air," Paulie said.

Azzecca picked up the airlines folder, pulled out the ticket, and looked at the passenger's name.

"Ah yes," he said, "Benny Napkins."

10: THE JACKASS

Carmine Ganucci could not fall asleep again.

The more he thought about the deal Truffatore and Ladruncolo had proposed, the more it stunk. To begin with, despite his fancy maneuvering, the profit was still very low. On an investment of fifty thousand dollars, he would earn a profit of thirty thousand dollars when the gold medallions were delivered to New York. *If* the medallions were delivered. And *if* they were really gold. Because if they weren't, he'd lose the whole fifty grand outright and besides have cleanup work to do in Naples, which meant hiring people you didn't know and trusting your business to strangers. But even if the medallions were really silver-plated gold, and even if they were delivered to New York, he would have all the trouble of melting them down and then getting rid of the gold, which seemed like an operation for a jeweler and not a respectable businessman. If he loan-sharked that same amount of money, the interest would be twenty per cent a week. At the end of four weeks, he could realize a profit of forty thousand dollars, ten thousand more than the Naples deal would bring. And it was more convenient to be dealing with people in New York, where if they didn't pay back the money, or if something else went wrong, you could always break their heads. And also, suppose those two Neapolitan morons got busted for bringing dope into Italy inside pearls, and suppose it got traced back to Carmine Ganucci, that he was responsible for the whole transaction, having provided the fifty G's that made the deal viable, so then he would be connected to an international dope smuggling operation, wonderful. And also, was it a sin to melt down medallions of the Virgin Mary?

The whole thing stunk.

"Carmine?" Stella said.

"What?"

"Are you asleep?"

"No."

"What are you doing?"

"Thinking."

"Thinking?" Stella said.

"Yes. I have to send another cable in the morning. Jesus," he said, "this is going to cost me a fortune."

"What kind of a cable?" Stella asked.

"To my lawyers. To tell them to never mind."

"Never mind what?"

"Never *mind* what," Ganucci said. "Also, we have to get in touch with a travel agent."

"Why?"

"Because I'm sick of this place and I want to go home and develop some of these pictures I've been taking."

Stella held her breath for just an instant and then, in a very small voice, asked, "When, Carmine?"

"Tomorrow," he said.

* * *

The night had turned hot and muggy.

All up and down the street, bare-armed women sat on front stoops and discussed the possibility of rain, while in the pizza parlor near the corner, men in shirt sleeves threw fingers at each other, deciding by the number showing on an outflung hand who would be Boss and who would be Under-Boss, who could drink beer and who could not.

Above the pizzeria, in Celia Mescolata's kitchen, Benny Napkins was winning a fortune and wishing that The Jackass would get hit by a bus. The very thought of winning from such expert gamblers as Celia and the men in her kitchen was dizzying. Even though it had been necessary to find a last-minute replacement for Willie, who had never shown up (and this was a definite loss since Willie was reputed to be a very shrewd gambler, the originator in fact of the Hong Kong Cut), these four men and Celia were as classy a collection of poker players as Benny had ever seen assembled. Each of them appreciated the solemn, almost religious nature of the game and each was willing to lose or win enormous sums of money with all the dignity of a priest at the poor box.

Even Celia, who had been reluctant to organize the game, and who was now losing as heavily as the men at the table, seemed to be enjoying the electric excitement with which bets were made and called, hands bluffed, pots escalated. Celia's game was blackjack, and she had told Benny flat out that afternoon that, as far as she was concerned, poker was always a losing proposition. The way she figured it (and she had spent a great deal of time figuring it, even though she could never master algebra at Julia Richman High School, which she had attended as a girl), the odds in blackjack were always in favor of the house because the dealer collected from players who went bust the *moment* they went bust, regardless of whether the dealer went bust later. Celia had painstakingly calculated that the odds (even after paying off for natural 21-counts, and adjusting for ties and standoffs) were almost six per cent in the dealer's favor. That was better than a person could get from most savings banks. That was why she liked blackjack. On the few occasions when poker had been played in her kitchen, she had cut the pot for ten per cent each hand, which to the casual onlooker might have seemed like a better percentage than six per cent. But Celia had estimated that she could deal six black-jack hands in the time it took to play one poker hand. When she multiplied her six per cent by six, it came to thirty-six as against ten per cent for cutting the poker pot, or so she calculated. She preferred blackjack.

But Benny Napkins had convinced her that this was to be no penny-ante, Cheap Charlie affair. In addition to himself, he wanted her to come up with five players who were willing to invest ten thousand dollars each in a freewheeling, old-fashioned, table-stakes poker game. It did not take Celia long to reckon that six times ten thousand was sixty thousand, and that the house cut on the total sum invested would be six thousand dollars. Even if she decided to play herself (which she had) and even if she lost her entire stake (which she did not plan to do), her total investment would be no more than four thousand dollars as against the possibility of winning fifty thousand dollars. That came to odds of at least twelve-and-a-half-to-one in her favor which were not as good as the thirty-six-percent blackjack take, but which were certainly better than the normal ten-per-cent poker take. Or so Celia reasoned.

In the meantime, Benny Napkins was winning. It was five minutes to ten, and he was winning. This was table-stakes poker and each player, at the start of the game, had placed in front of him a ten-thousand-dollar bundle. (No one had actually *counted* the bills in each bundle, but Benny presumed the other players were at least slightly more honest than he and had brought into the game the price of admission as announced by Celia Mescolata.) He glanced around the table now as Ricco Locare, who was Willie's replacement, dealt the cards. Benny's quick estimate was that he had at least thirty thousand dollars in bills of various denominations sitting in front of him, whereas the other players' piles had diminished respectively and noticeably.

It was now three minutes to ten, and Ricco was telling Celia to bet her ace.

Oh, please, Benny thought, *if there is a God in heaven, please let The Jackass break his leg.*

"Hundred for the ace," Celia said.

"I'll see you," Morrie Goldstein said.

"Benny?"

"Raise it a hundred," Benny said.

"What've you got there, a lousy pair of jacks?" Celia said, looking over at the open jack of diamonds.

"Be three of them on the next card," Benny said, and grinned.

It was two minutes to ten.

"Two hundred to you, Angie," Ricco said.

"Call."

"I'll take a chance too," Ricco said, and anted, and then turned to the player on his left. "What do you say, Ralph?"

"What the hell," Ralph said, and put his two hundred in the pot.

"Here we go," Ricco said, and began dealing.

He gave Benny his third jack just as the hands on Celia's kitchen clock reached the hour. Benny closed his eyes, and opened them again in the next instant, when the kitchen door was kicked in. A tall skinny man with a nylon stocking pulled over his face (always a goddamn nylon stocking,

Benny thought, and sighed) and a stupid white hat pulled low on his forehead and a forty-five automatic pistol in his fist, barged into the room and said, "Don't nobody move," the automatic covering the table like a cannon over the Strait of Gibraltar. Nobody moved. Everybody knew better than to move because, with the possible exception of Celia, each of the players in the game had occasionally been on the *other* end of a cannon pointing at somebody, and they knew it was prudent not to move in such circumstances. So the tall skinny man with the stocking over his head moved swiftly around the table and scooped up all of the money there— exactly fifty-two thousand dollars, since at least some of the players were just as dishonest as Benny and had brought into the game less than the required admission stake. The man with the stocking over his head put all of the money into a large A & P shopping bag, and then backed toward the door, still waving the automatic.

He slammed the door behind him.

Benny Napkins wanted to weep.

Detective Lieutenant Alexander Bozzaris was heading up the street for Celia Mescolata's apartment—where he intended to bust the card game unless the players took up a collection in his honor—when he saw a tall skinny guy running in his direction. The guy had a nylon stocking pulled over his head and a shopping bag in his hands. It looked as if dollar bills were spilling out of the shopping bag. Bozzaris right away figured something was up.

"Stop!" he yelled. "Police!"

11: DOMINICK THE GURU

Dominick was wearing a plaid shirt, blue jeans, brown cotton gloves, and black track shoes, his usual working uniform. In his right hand he carried a black leather bag containing the tools of his trade, namely: a hand drill and bits of various sizes, a jimmy, a complete set of picklocks, several punches and skeleton keys, a pair of nippers, a hacksaw, and a crowbar designed so that it could be taken apart and carried in three sections. Slung over his left shoulder was a laundry bag full of various items he had collected that night. The combined weight of the two bags made it somewhat difficult to negotiate the iron rungs of the fire escapes running up the rear wall of the building. But then, every occupation has its hazards.

Dominick had cased the building for three weeks running, and had decided that tonight, Thursday, would be a good time for a hit. Thursday night was maid's night off, which meant that a lot of the tenants went out to eat, which further meant that their apartments would be empty for long stretches at a time. Dominick was a careful worker and did not like to be interrupted unexpectedly. It was now a little past ten-thirty, and he had worked three apartments already and was thinking that perhaps he ought to head for home. But he was still feeling energetic and, in fact, invigorated (it was funny the way breaking and entry could buoy up a man's sagging spirits), and so he decided to rip off one more place before retiring for the night. The apartment he chose was on the tenth floor rear, with the fire escape just outside a darkened window. The room was not air-conditioned; the window was wide open. Dominick could only assume that the tenants were out-of-towners who had just moved to New York.

He crouched on the fire escape for a long time, peering into the room. The door leading to the rest of the apartment was closed, and so it was impossible to tell whether or not anyone was in one of the other rooms. But he could hear no sounds, could see no telltale sliver of light showing in the crack at the bottom of the closed door. He eased himself into the room and padded across it in his track shoes. He put his ear against the door and listened. He could still hear nothing. Satisfied, he took a small flashlight from his pocket and looked around.

The room was a bedroom, *not* the master bedroom, worse luck. Single bed against the wall, framed print over it. Worthless. Dresser on the opposite wall, small alarm clock on its top. Likewise worthless. Easy chair and ottoman near a closed door, probably a closet. Dominick opened the door and flashed the light inside. Three empty wire hangers. Great. On the shelf over the bar, a fishing creel and a man's gray fedora. He was beginning to think he should have quit when he was ahead, and was moving toward the door again, about to explore the rest of the apartment, when he heard voices in the corridor outside. He ducked quickly into the closet, barely getting the door closed before the lights in the room snapped on.

"Why can't I stay up to watch Johnny Carson?" a boy's voice asked.

"Because it's time you went to bed," a woman's voice said.

"My mother lets me stay up till twelve," the boy said.

"That's a lie. Besides, your mother isn't here."

"It's the truth, I swear."

Boy, what bullshit, Dominick thought.

"Could I have a glass of milk?" the boy asked.

"You've already had a glass of milk," the woman answered.

Tell him, Dominick thought. *Put the little bastard to bed.*

"I want you to say your prayers and then get under the covers," the woman said.

Dominick heard some movement outside, probably the kid shuffling over to the side of the bed and getting on his knees. *Boy, what bullshit,* he thought.

"Now I lay me down to sleep," the boy said, "I pray the Lord my soul to keep. If I should die before I wake, I pray the Lord my soul to take. Bless Mama and Papa."

Dominick shrugged. Some more shuffling outside, the sound of bedsprings creaking as the kid climbed in.

"Good night now," the woman said.

"Good night," the boy said.

Footsteps going to the door.

"I forgot to take off my watch," the boy said. "I don't like to hear it ticking when I sleep."

Good, Dominick thought. *Take it off and kiss it good-by.*

Footsteps coming past the closet to the bed again. Footsteps going from the bed across the room to the dresser. Footsteps going to the door again.

"Good night, Ida."

Good night already, Dominick thought.

"Good night, Lewis," the woman said.

Click, the room lights going out, the narrow ribbon of light at the bottom of the closet door disappearing. The sound of the bedroom door easing shut. Silence. Dominick waited in the darkness thinking he could've been home in bed screwing Virginia, instead of standing here with his neck all cramped up against a shelf. Still, the watch might be worth something.

He waited in the darkness for at least a half hour, hoping the kid would fall asleep fast. At last, he eased the closet door open a crack and listened. He heard the sounds of even breathing from the bed. He opened the door a bit wider, listened for another five minutes, and then decided to chance it. Tiptoeing across the room, he felt along the dresser top and picked up the watch without even looking at it. He was out the window in a wink, laundry bag slung over his left shoulder, burglar's tools clutched tightly in his right hand, the watch safely tucked into one pocket of his blue jeans. He did not look at the watch until he got back to his own apartment at ten minutes to midnight.

Dominick yawned, put the watch back in his pocket, and went to sleep.

12: FREDDIE

Mario Azzecca's messenger was a man named Freddie Corriere. He had been summoned to the Sutton Place apartment at nine-thirty, had received his instructions from the lawyer, and had proceeded immediately and promptly to Benny Napkins' place on Twenty-fourth Street. Neither Benny nor Jeanette Kay was home, so Freddie went downstairs and made a phone call from the booth on the corner, advising Azzecca of the situation and asking for further instructions. Azzecca told him to keep trying even if it took all night.

By twelve-thirty, Freddie had been back to the apartment a total of four additional times. Benny lived on the fifth floor in a building that didn't have an elevator. Climbing five flights of stairs, up and down, five times in the course of two and a half hours could cause severe thirst in a person. Fortunately, there was a bar on Twenty-fifth Street, so that Freddie could rest in a nice sociable atmosphere between his visits to Benny's building. By twelve-thirty, he had consumed six scotches plus one bottle of beer. He had ordered another beer, and had promised himself that he would go back to the apartment again at one A.M., as soon as he finished the second beer.

That was when Sarah came into the bar.

Freddie knew Sarah from when she used to work for Bobby Mezzano up on Forty-ninth Street. She was a big tall black girl with a bushy head of hair and bright white teeth, and also very nice breasts. She was wearing a tight-fitting silk jersey dress and, because it was summertime, and also because of the nature of her profession, she didn't have anything on under the dress. Freddie noticed this at once.

"Hello there, Sarah," he said, "what brings you here to this part of town?"

"Who's that?" Sarah asked, and peered into the darkness toward the end of the bar where Freddie sat nursing his beer.

"Me," he said, "Freddie Corriere."

"Freddie, hey there," she said, and walked over. "Buy a girl a drink?"

"Sure," Freddie said, and snapped his fingers at the bartender. "What's your pleasure?"

"That's what *I'm* supposed to ask," Sarah said, and laughed.

"Oh," Freddie said. "Yeah." He laughed with her. He hadn't quite caught her little joke, but what the hell. "Anyway," he said, "what would you like to drink?"

"A vermouth cassis," Sarah said.

"Yeah?" Freddie said.

"What are you having?" the bartender said, walking over.

"A vermouth cassis," Sarah repeated.

The bartender looked at her malevolently for a moment, shook his head, and walked away to mix the drink.

"I never had one of those, those vermouth cassises," Freddie said.

"They're very nice. You should try one," Sarah said. "I'll give you a little sip of mine when it comes. Would you like a little sip of mine?"

"Yeah," Freddie said, and looked up at the wall clock. It was twenty minutes to one. "Anyway," he said, "what are you doing down around here? I thought you worked uptown."

"Where there's occupation, I occupy myself," Sarah said.

"Yeah?" Freddie said.

"Yeah," Sarah said.

"One vermouth cassis," the bartender said. "Only we ain't got no cassis, so it's only vermouth."

"What's that, that cassis?" Freddie asked.

"It's a liqueur," Sarah said.

"Yeah?"

"Yeah," the bartender said, "only we ain't got none." He looked at Sarah malevolently again, and then went to the other end of the bar to watch television.

"Guess nothing's gonna go right tonight," Sarah said, and lifted her glass. "Cheers," she said.

"*Salute,*" Freddie said. It was one of the two Italian words he knew. The other one was "*Vanapoli,*" which was three words in itself, but Freddie didn't realize that. "Anyway, what else went wrong tonight?" he asked.

"Everything," Sarah said, and swallowed a gulp of vermouth, and then put down the glass and lighted a cigarette. "I was supposed to meet a guy down here at midnight. He never showed."

"Yeah?" Freddie said,

"Yeah. Got the room and everything."

"Yeah?" Freddie said.

"Yeah," Sarah said.

"I don't see why nobody would stand you up, Sarah," he said. "Good-looking girl like you."

"Well, honey, somebody just did," Sarah said, and blew out a stream of smoke, and lifted her glass. "It's a shame, too, because I already paid for the room and all."

"Yeah?" Freddie said, and looked up at the wall clock again. It was ten minutes to one.

"Yeah," Sarah said. "Oh well," she said, and swallowed another gulp of vermouth. "What gets me is the room going to waste all night, that's what gets me."

"Where *is* that room?" Freddie asked.

"On Twenty-first."

"Yeah?" Freddie said.

"Yeah."

"That ain't too far from here."

"It's practically around the corner," Sarah said, and crossed her legs.

"I have to make a delivery on Twenty-fourth and Third," Freddie said.

"Yeah?"

"Yeah. But after that, I'm free the rest of the night," Freddie said. "If I wanted to lay you," he said subtly, "how much would it cost?"

"Well, I already paid for the room, you know."

"Yeah, how much is that?"

"Twelve dollars."

"Yeah?"

"Yeah."

"And how much are you?"

"I'm twenty-five."

"Yeah?"

"Yeah," Sarah said.

"So that comes to an even thirty-eight dollars."

"Thirty-seven dollars," Sarah said.

"Twelve and twenty-five," Freddie said, and added silently in his head. "Right, thirty-seven. That's not so bad."

"No, that's not so bad. Some of the girls are getting a lot more."

"Yeah?" Freddie said.

"Yeah."

"Well, listen, would you like to walk me over to Twenty-fourth while I make this delivery, and then we can go over to that room, okay?"

"Sounds good to me," Sarah said.

"Yeah?"

"Yeah," she said.

Freddie paid for the drinks, and they walked to Twenty-fourth Street, where Sarah waited downstairs for him, and where he again climbed the five flights to Benny Napkins' apartment. Nobody was home. He went downstairs again, puffing hard. Sarah was leaning against the building, smoking.

"Everything taken care of?" she asked.

"No, nobody's still there," he said.

"Well, you can take care of it later, huh?"

"Yeah," Freddie said. "I tried, didn't I?"

"Sure, you did. Right now you're gonna take care of *me*, huh?"

"Yeah?" Freddie said.

They walked away from the building arm-in-arm. Ten minutes later, Benny Napkins pulled up in a cab with Jeanette Kay, whom he had picked up outside the Trans-Lux 85th Street. Jeanette Kay was anxious to get upstairs because *Crime of Passion*, with Barbara Stanwyck and Sterling Hayden, was showing on Channel 5.

The Jackass refused to take off his stocking.

"That is a mask," Bozzaris told him, "and there are laws against people wearing masks."

"It's not a mask, it's a garment."

"Be that as it may, it is still a mask," Bozzaris said.

"It's a stocking," The Jackass said.

"If you wear it over your face, it's a mask."

"If you wear a mask on your foot, does that make it a stocking?" The Jackass asked.

"Don't be a wise guy," Bozzaris said.

"I know my rights," The Jackass said, because whereas he was not too terribly bright, his empirical knowledge of criminal law was formidable and impressive.

"Be that as it may," Bozzaris said, and decided then and there to advise him of his rights, it being the habit of bums all over these days to complain that this or that thing was not done according to the book. "In keeping with the Supreme Court decision in *Miranda versus Arizona*," he said, "we're required to advise you of your rights, and that's what I'm doing now."

"Correct," The Jackass said approvingly.

"First, you have the right to remain silent, if you choose, do you understand that?"

"Correct, and I do."

"Do you also understand that you need not answer any police questions?"

"Correct, and I do."

"And do you also understand that if you *do* answer questions . . ."

". . . my answers may be used as evidence against me, correct. I understand."

"I must also inform you that you have the right to consult with an attorney before or during police questioning, do you understand that?"

"Yes," The Jackass said, "and I also understand that if I decide to exercise that right but do not have the funds with which to hire counsel, I am entitled to have a lawyer appointed without cost, to consult with him before or during questioning."

"Correct," Bozzaris said.

"Do you understand all of your rights?" The Jackass asked.

"I do," Bozzaris said.

"Do you want a lawyer?" The Jackass asked.

"What?" Bozzaris said, and blinked, and then narrowed his eyes. "Listen," he said, "don't be a wise guy. The last wise guy we had in here is right this minute languishing in the Tombs."

"I want a lawyer," The Jackass said.

"Do you have any special lawyer in mind?"

"I do."

"Who?"

"Mario Azzecca," The Jackass said, and Bozzaris suddenly sniffed the sweet scent of money wafting on the stale squad-room air.

Azzecca was in bed with his wife Sybil when the telephone rang at two o'clock in the morning. He immediately knew it was trouble. His son up at Harvard had undoubtedly been busted on a Possession of Marijuana charge, little bastard.

"Hello?" he said.

"Lieutenant Bozzaris here," the voice on the other end said. "There is something important we have to discuss."

"At two o'clock in the morning?" Azzecca said.

"Who is it?" his wife asked.

"Go to sleep," Azzecca said. "Hold on a minute," he said to Bozzaris, "I want to take this in my study." He got out of bed in his pajamas, put on a dressing gown, and went out of the bedroom and down the corridor to where Sybil—out of the goodness of her miserly heart—had provided him with an eight-by-ten work space in a twelve-room apartment. He picked up the extension phone and said, "What's so important, Lieutenant?"

"Money," Bozzaris said.

"What are you talking about?"

"I'm talking about somewhere in the vicinity of fifty thousand dollars that is now in our possession," Bozzaris said.

The telephone began shaking in Azzecca's hand. "What about it?" he said calmly.

"Our information leads us to believe that maybe this money is earmarked for one Carmine Ganucci in Naples," Bozzaris said, and Azzecca immediately realized that Freddie Corriere, that dumb bastard, had somehow got himself picked up on the way to Benny Napkins' place.

"Your information is wrong," Azzecca answered, because why had Bozzaris said "in the *vicinity* of fifty thousand dollars?" What vicinity? Corriere had been carrying *exactly* fifty thousand dollars in an envelope with a rubber band around it, not to mention the airline ticket to Naples.

"Be that as it may," Bozzaris said, "I have no desire to interfere in the various activities or industries you fellows are engaged or involved in, so long as they are not criminal in nature, or evil in intent. You may recall that not too long ago, some of my fellows picked up a worthless batch of figures which were meaningless to us and certainly not indicative of any crime being committed, so we returned them to their rightful owner, namely one Joseph Dirigere who, in gratitude, contributed seven thousand four hundred dollars to the squad's pension and retirement fund."

"I remember," Azzecca said.

"I thought you might," Bozzaris said. "Now, similarly and likewise, I have no way of knowing whether this currency is what is sometimes referred to as tainted money, or bad money, or dirty money, I have no way of knowing that. In looking it over, it seems to me like just any normal kind of money, which is neither clean nor dirty, but just plain cold hard cash." Bozzaris paused. "On the barrelhead."

"How much?" Azzecca said.

"Same as last time," Bozzaris answered at once.

"Too much," Azzecca said.

"All right, all right, who wants to haggle where hardworking policemen are involved? Make it an even five thousand."

"Ridiculous," Azzecca said.

"I'm willing to compromise," Bozzaris said. "Thirty-five hundred."

"Two thousand."

"Twenty-five hundred?"

"Two thousand," Azzecca said, "and not a penny more."

"It's a deal," Bozzaris said. "Where shall I send your man with the remainder of the cash?"

"Freddie?"

"Is that his name? He ain't told us a thing. And, also, he's got a goddamn stocking pulled over his head."

"I always knew he was a little queer," Azzecca said.

"Be that as it may," Bozzaris said, "shall I send him over to your place after we make the agreed-upon deduction at this end?"

"Yes. But tell him to leave the package with the doorman."

"The doorman? Don't you want him to come upstairs?"

"If he comes upstairs, I'm liable to strangle him with my bare hands, right here in my own living room," Azzecca said.

"I'll make believe I didn't hear that," Bozzaris said, and chuckled. "Nice talking to you."

"Send the *ticket* back, too," Azzecca said.

But Bozzaris had already hung up.

At twenty minutes to three, the buzzer in Azzecca's kitchen sounded while he was sitting at the table drinking a glass of milk. He went swiftly to the wall and pressed the TALK toggle.

"Yes?" he said.

"Mr. Azzecca, this is Hymie on the door. I got a package for you."

"Send it right up," Azzecca said.

"Fellow who delivered it said it was important, so I didn't know whether I should wait till morning . . ."

"Yes, yes, send it right up," Azzecca said.

". . . or buzz you now in the middle of the night. *Should* I send it up?"

"Please," Azzecca said.

The elevator operator knocked on the door five minutes later and handed Azzecca an A & P shopping bag. Azzecca thanked him, closed and locked the door, and then went into the living room, wondering how come the money had been transferred to a shopping bag from a plain white envelope with a rubber band around it. He turned the bag over, dumped its contents onto the coffee table, and wondered how come the fifty thousand dollars had been in hundred-dollar denominations when it *left* this apartment, whereas it *now* seemed to be in various denominations—tens, twenties, singles, *and* century notes.

He began counting the money.

And then he began wondering why Lieutenant Bozzaris, after his long song and dance on the telephone, had not bothered after all to deduct the two-thousand-dollar contribution to his squad's pension and retirement fund.

The bills on Azzecca's living room coffee table added up to exactly fifty thousand dollars, the identical amount that Freddie Corriere had carried out of here at 9:45 P.M. Bozzaris had deducted the ticket to Naples, but that was all. Maybe he was planning on taking a little trip.

Azzecca shrugged.

Tomorrow, he would have to send another messenger to

Benny Napkins. By then, he figured he would have heard from the good lieutenant again, correcting his oversight. Azzecca belched, finished his glass of milk, and went to bed with his ulcer growling nonetheless.

13: BLOOMINGDALES

Benny Napkins was asleep when his doorbell sounded at ten o'clock Friday morning. He got out of bed, being very careful not to disturb Jeanette Kay, and then went through the apartment to the front door.

"Who is it?" he asked.

"Freddie Corriere."

Benny lifted the peephole flap and peered into the hallway. It was indeed Freddie Corriere, looking wan and exhausted and skinnier than usual, but Freddie Corriere nonetheless. Benny unlocked both Segal locks, slipped the Fox lock bar to the floor, undid the night chain, and opened the door.

"Okay to come in?" Freddie asked.

"Yes, sure, but please be very quiet as Jeanette Kay is still asleep."

"Yeah?" Freddie said.

"Yeah," Benny said.

"I was supposed to bring this to you last night," Freddie said, "but I kept trying here, and nobody was home."

"I was at a card game," Benny said, "and Jeanette Kay went to the movies."

"Yeah?" Freddie said. "Did you win?"

"In a manner of speaking," Benny said, and sighed.

"I had a very interesting time last night," Freddie said, anxious to tell someone, if only Benny Napkins, of the marvelous things he and Sarah had done together.

"I had a very interesting time too," Benny said, "but I haven't got time to discuss it right now. I got to get dressed and go up to Harlem for the work, and also there's some other pressing matters I have to attend to."

"Oh, sure," Freddie said. "Maybe some other time."

"What's this?" Benny said, and looked at the bulging envelope in his hands.

"It's from Mario Azzecca," Freddie said. "There's instructions inside."

"Did you read the instructions?"

"Would I read something marked personal to you?"

"I guess not," Benny said.

"Also, I can't read," Freddie said, and shrugged.

"Well, thank you for bringing it over," Benny said. "I'd offer you a cup of coffee, but Jeanette Kay is still asleep, and I like her to sleep herself out."

"Oh, sure," Freddie said. "Some other time, maybe. Then maybe we can also discuss this girl I had last night who . . ."

"Some other time," Benny said.

"Yeah," Freddie said, and left the apartment.

Benny sighed and went into the kitchen. He put down the bulging envelope, afraid to open it because he was certain that anything from Mario Azzecca would only be some new calamity. He put the coffeepot on the stove, sat down at the kitchen table, and stared at the envelope. He was surprised that The Jackass had not contacted him after last night's stickup, but maybe The Jackass had decided to take a plane to India or someplace. If there was one thing you could never trust it was a crook, especially if he happened to be a dumb one. The Jackass had probably never seen that kind of money in his entire life; it was easy to imagine it going to his head. Benny could visualize him taking off all his clothes, except the stocking, and then laying down naked on his bed and rubbing himself all over with those crisp green bills. And then he had probably got on a plane to India.

Benny wished *he* was on a plane to India.

He had been that close, *that* close, to getting the ransom money legitimately, if only The Jackass hadn't been such a jackass. But then again, he himself was the one who'd figured out the heist, so he couldn't very well blame the poor soul, who'd only followed instructions—except that the poor soul was a very larcenous bastard who had probably decided to keep all the marbles for himself. Well, we all make mistakes, Benny thought. Like that time in Chicago, he thought, and looked at the envelope again, and wondered what kind of trouble Azzecca was sending him on a nice Friday morning.

The coffeepot was perking. Benny got a cup and saucer from the cabinet and set it on the kitchen table. He kept stealing sidelong glances at the envelope each time he passed it, as though by constantly referring to it, it might miraculously disappear.

The time in Chicago was a very natural mistake, Benny thought. Why can't they ever let a man forget things? He poured coffee from the pot and looked at the envelope again. How was he supposed to know that the man who was opening Domizio's Italian Restaurant was none other than Carmine Ganucci's brother? Benny had followed the same routine he always did when a new restaurant was opening in Chicago. He had paid a visit to the establishment and casually mentioned that several interested parties would like to collect the garbage and supply the linen. Domizio had said, "Get the hell out of here, Dummy." So that night some of Benny's friends had inadvertently thrown a garbage can through the new plateglass window of Domizio's splendid establishment. It really served Domizio right, because if a man's name was Domizio Ganucci, he shouldn't go changing it to Domizio Galsworthy, what the hell kind of a name was that for a man running an Italian restaurant? And with a fabulous heritage like his? A member of the Ganucci family? Sometimes Benny simply couldn't understand people's motivations. *What's in a name?* he quoted silently, *That which we call a rose by any other name would smell as sweet,* and then shrugged and thought, *Rose is a rose is a rose is a rose,* no?, and tried to consider the more fortunate aspects of the episode, the most felicitous of which had been the fact that he hadn't woken up in the Chicago Sanitary and Ship Canal the next morning.

Instead, Carmine Ganucci had arrived personally from New York to report that he understood the mistake, of course, it was an honest mistake, but the plate-glass window had cost his dear brother Domizio one thousand two hundred and fifty dollars, and this amount would be deducted from the money due Benny as his percentage of the garbage and linen business. In the future, however, Benny would no longer be getting a percentage from that profession. Instead, Benny was being asked to transfer to New York, where there was an excellent opening for a salaried pickup man in East Harlem, if Benny was interested in the job. The position would not pay as much as he was accustomed to earning, but Benny had to understand that plate-glass windows did not grow on trees. And whereas the entire incident had certainly been highly amusing, it was also pretty damn stupid to try to shake down the brother of Carmine Ganucci, did Benny think he understood that?

Benny thought he did.

He thanked Ganucci for allowing him the opportunity to work in a nice city like New York, especially in a nice location like East Harlem, and then he took a walk over to Thirty-first Street, and looked down at the canal and said ten *Hail Marys,* aloud, to make sure somebody heard him.

We all make mistakes, he thought, but it did seem he was making more than his share of them lately. He should have told Nanny that she had picked someone who was really *too* small a potato to be handling the job of getting back Ganucci's little bastard of a kid. That was what he should have done in the beginning. But, failing that, he should never have tried something as stupid as holding up a card game, especially when somebody as dumb and as sneaky as The Jackass was involved. He wondered where that dumb, sneaky jackass was right this very minute, and then he looked at Azzecca's ominous envelope and decided he had better open it and find out what was in store for him. He still had $216.00 in the bank, and that would certainly take him to Schenectady at least, if not Hawaii or India. Benny had an aunt in Schenectady who ran a hero stand.

He sipped some more coffee, put down the coffee cup, apprehensively picked up the envelope, and slid off the rubber band.

There seemed to be fifty thousand dollars in the envelope, in hundred-dollar bills.

There also seemed to be a round-trip ticket to Naples in the envelope.

And also a letter:

AZZECCA AND GARBUGLI
ATTORNEYS AT LAW

TELEPHONE (212) CO 5-3598
CABLE: AZZGAR

145 WEST 45 STREET
NEW YORK, N. Y. 10036

Benny Napkins:

Get on this plane Friday night at ten. Go
to Naples. (Don't forget to change in Rome.)
Give this money to Ganucci's messenger at the
Naples airport Saturday. Don't fuck up.

Mario Azzecca

MA/mp

Benny read the letter again. He counted the money again.
He looked at the ticket again. He now had the fifty thousand
dollars some madman of a kidnaper had demanded for the safe
return of Carmine Ganucci's son. The only trouble was Carmine Ganucci wanted the money taken to Naples.

For the second time in twelve hours, Benny wanted to weep.

The best fence in town was a man named Bloomingdales, not to
be confused with the store of the same name minus an apostro-
phe. Bloomingdales, the man, had an apartment on 116th Street,
just off Lexington Avenue, and it was conceivably the busiest
little bargain walk-up in all of East Harlem. People came from
near and far to view the merchandise on display in Bloomingdales' four-room railroad flat. It was rumored that Bloomingdales had once exhibited a stolen grand piano in his kitchen,

but Dominick the Guru had never actually seen the Steinway, and was disinclined to accept the story on faith alone. Dominick had, however, seen goods of every conceivable description in those four brimming rooms, and had on occasion been tempted to merely trade his own stolen merchandise for one or another item on display. Radios, television sets, toasters, gold watches, gold pen-and-pencil sets, stereos, umbrellas, cloth coats, fur coats, lamps, gold necklaces and rings, musical instruments, chessmen and boards, a complete set of the novels of Charles Dickens bound in hand-tooled leather, crystal, china, bicycles, tricycles, and once even a Honda, all of these and more, much more, could be found in Bloomingdales' upstairs bazaar at any day of the week, Saturdays and Sundays included. A person was unlikely to discover silver watches, rings or necklaces, sterling flatware or even silver plate in Bloomingdales' stock because he generally laid such items off on The Silver Fox, who was expert at determining their value, and who catered to a clientele exclusively interested in sauceboats, ladles, serving platters and other silver pieces in any shape or size. But anything else, ranging from the smallest transistor to the largest combination washer-dryer, with prices starting as low as five dollars and ten cents, and soaring as high as three thousand dollars (the reputed asking price for the Steinway Dominick had never seen) was available to the bargain hunter who didn't mind running the risk of being charged with violation of Section 1306 of the New York State Penal Law, succinctly defined as *Buying, receiving, concealing or withholding stolen or wrongfully acquired property.* Moreover, the thieves themselves—shoplifters, pickpockets, burglars, and assorted holdup men and robbers—found it rewarding to deal with Bloomingdales because he was uncompromisingly honest, and paid top dollar besides for whatever they brought to him. The only complaint Dominick had was that Bloomingdales was all the time yelling about his appearance.

"Why don't you cut your hair?" Bloomingdales said. "Nice Italian boy like you."

"I like my hair this way," Dominick said.

"You look like a pansy queer," Bloomingdales said.

"Lots of girls like the way I look with my hair this way," Dominick said.

"Lots of girls are crazy, too," Bloomingdales said. "Why don't you get a nice haircut like mine?"

"Well, that *is* a nice haircut," Dominick said, "but I like the way *I* look, too."

"You look like a fruit faggot," Bloomingdales said.

"Well, lots of girls think I look very masculine with my hair this way."

"Lots of girls are crazy bull dyke daggers, too," Bloomingdales said. "You're a very good burglar, why do you have to wear your hair like that?"

"Well, you want to look at what I brought you?" Dominick asked.

"You know who wears their hair like that?" Bloomingdales asked.

"Who?"

"Crazy fruit pansy faggot queer freaks, that's who," Bloomingdales said.

"I got a lot of nice things here," Dominick said, and opened the large suitcase he had carried up the three flights to Bloomingdales' apartment. True to his word, he did have a lot of nice things there, including a tortoise-shell comb-and-brush set, a large diamond engagement ring, a radio-alarm clock, a gold choker, a silver tea service . . .

"I don't take silver," Bloomingdales said.

"I thought you might be able to lay it off on The Silver Fox. Isn't that what you usually do?"

"Usually. But we had a few words, The Silver Fox and me.

"I'm sorry to hear that," Dominick said.

"Mmm," Bloomingdales said. "He called my sister a no-good whore."

"Why, she's a very *good* whore," Dominick said.

"Don't I know it? So where does he come off casting aspersions?"

"Well, everybody's a little crazy every now and then," Dominick said.

"The Silver Fox is crazy *all* the time, you ask me," Bloomingdales said. "Anyway, I don't take silver no more. This, this, this, and this you'll have to bring to him directly."

"How much for all the other stuff?" Dominick asked.

Bloomingdales opened a drawer in a cabinet against the wall, one of the few legitimately purchased pieces in his apartment. He withdrew from it an adding machine that had been stolen from Goldsmith Bros., and quickly ran off a tape. He studied the tape, looked over the material again, nodded, hit another set of tabs, pulled the lever again, looked at the tape again, and said, "Two hundred and six dollars for the lot." He looked up at Dominick. "Excluding the engagement ring, which I want to have appraised a little before I set a price on it."

"At least give me an estimate," Dominick said.

"I think maybe it's worth another two bills to me, I'll let you know."

"I thought maybe three," Dominick said.

"Maybe," Bloomingdales said dubiously. "You going to see The Silver Fox with the rest of this?"

"Later today," Dominick said.

"Tell him I hope he gets run over by a subway, that bastard."

"I'll tell him," Dominick said. He put the silver items back into the suitcase, closed it, and then waited while Bloomingdales counted out two hundred and six dollars in crisp new bills;

Bloomingdales always paid off in crisp new bills, which was another reason it was so nice to do business with him.

On the sidewalk downstairs, Dominick realized he had not shown Bloomingdales the watch that was still in the pocket of his blue jeans. He debated going all the way upstairs again, and then figured the hell with it.

At 12:35 P.M. that Friday afternoon, just as Dominick was walking away from Bloomingdales' building, a trusted messenger was arriving at Benny Napkins' place further downtown. He climbed the five flights of stairs, walked down the hall, and, wheezing, knocked on Benny's door.

"Who is it?" Benny asked.

"Me," the messenger said. "Arthur Doppio."

"What do you want, Arthur?" Benny asked.

"I have something for you," Arthur said.

"What do you have?" Benny asked.

"Something from Mario Azzecca," Arthur said.

Benny lifted the peephole flap, peered into the hallway and saw Arthur holding up a sealed white envelope with a rubber band around it. "Just a second," Benny said. He unlocked both Segal locks, slid the bar of the Fox lock to the floor, took off the night chain, and opened the door.

"Aren't you going to ask me in?" Arthur said.

"I would," Benny answered, "but Jeanette Kay is asleep, and I like her to sleep till she's all slept out." Even as the words left his mouth, Benny had the feeling he had lived through this identical life experience before, in the not too distant past. He took the bulging white envelope from Arthur's hand. The envelope had a familiar feel to it.

"Well, some other time, then," Arthur said, and tipped his hat and walked away down the corridor. Benny closed and locked the door. The feeling of *déjà vu* persisted. *It seems,* he quoted silently, *we stood and talked like this before, we looked at each other in the same way then, but I can't remember where or when,* nor could he remember the rest of the song. He took the envelope into the kitchen, sat down at the table, and stared at the envelope for several moments, wondering what new trouble Mario Azzecca was sending him. At last he sighed, slipped the rubber band off the envelope, and ripped open the flap.

There seemed to be fifty thousand dollars in the envelope, in bills of various denominations.

There also seemed to be a round-trip ticket to Naples in the envelope.

And also a letter:

AZZECCA AND GARBUGLI
ATTORNEYS AT LAW

TELEPHONE (212) CO 5-3598   145 WEST 45 STREET
CABLE: AZZGAR   NEW YORK, N. Y. 10036

```
         Benny Napkins:

         Get on this plane Friday night at ten.  Go
         to Naples.  (Don't forget to change in Rome.)
         Give this money to Ganucci's messenger at the
         Naples airport Saturday.  Don't fuck up.


                       Mario Azzecca
         MA/mp
```

Benny read the letter again. He counted the money again. He looked at the ticket again.

He could only figure that somehow the computer had broke down.

14: THE SILVER FOX

Spectacles reflecting glints of silver plate and sterling, The Silver Fox sat behind a table stacked with stolen goods, and listened to Benny's lament. It was now almost 1:30 P.M., and the plane for Rome was scheduled to leave at ten.

"What am I supposed to do?" Benny asked.

He had come to see The Silver Fox because he considered him his oldest friend and most trusted adviser, even though he continued searching for hallmarks all the while they talked.

"We first have to eliminate what you *can't* do," The Silver Fox said. "That's the first thing we have to do."

"Okay, what is it I can't do?" Benny asked.

"You can't send the duplication back to Azzecca."

"Why not?"

"Nobody likes to be reminded that he made a mistake," The Silver Fox said.

"But this is a very *big* mistake," Benny said. "This is fifty thousand dollars involved here."

"The bigger the mistake, the more nobody wants to be reminded of it."

"I suppose that's true," Benny said.

"I remember one time," The Silver Fox said, "when my brother Salvatore, which means Our Lord Jesus Christ the Savior in Italian, made the terrible mistake of laying Paulie Secondo's arrangement who was living with him at that time on Greenwich Avenue, and the girl told Paulie about it even though she had been Irish and willing, and Paulie managed to hint to a police lieutenant he knows by the name of Alexander Bozzaris that my brother Salvatore had entertained a rape which was statutory, the girl having been only sixteen, and whereas they afterwards arrested him and he spent ten years in Sing Sing, and then when he got out somebody named Alonzo from Eighty-sixth Street made the terrible mistake of reminding my brother Salvatore that he had taken a fall for boffing that little girl, and whereas my brother cut him with a knife four times and was sent back to Sing Sing again. Nobody likes to be reminded of their mistakes, Benny."

"So what should I do?" Benny said.

"I have the feeling you're not telling me the whole story," The Silver Fox said wisely. "Otherwise, there is no question about what you should do. You should take one of those fifty-thousand-dollar bundles to Naples, and you should *spend* the other one. Mario Azzecca is never going to admit to anybody in the entire world that he made such a mistake, believe me."

"Suppose he does, Silvio? Suppose he comes to me and says he wants the money back?"

"So? Are you tongue-tied? Do you stutter? You tell him, *What* money? I got only one fifty-thousand-dollar bundle, which I took it to Naples like you told me, and I gave it to the guy I met at the airport, and I came back here, and here I am, so what money are you talking about? The money you are talking about has already been signed, sealed, and delivered. *That's* what you tell him. *If* he comes to see you. Whereas he won't anyway."

"Well, maybe," Benny said.

"No maybes." The Silver Fox raised his eyeglasses onto his forehead and peered across the table at Benny. "What is it you're withholding from me, Benny? I'm your friend, you can tell me."

"I don't want to get you involved, Silvio."

"Why not?"

"Because you *are* my friend, and this could mean trouble for the people involved."

"What are friends for," The Silver Fox asked, "if not to share each other's troubles?"

"No, please, I don't want to burden you."

"I'm your friend," The Silver Fox said. "Whatever it is, I'll try to help you."

"No," Benny said, shaking his head, "no, really."

"Tell me," The Silver Fox said. "You can trust me."

"Well . . ."

"Tell me."

"Well," Benny said, "Carmine Ganucci's son has been kidnaped."

"Why'd you tell me that?" The Silver Fox said, leaping to his feet. "You want to get me in trouble? What kind of friend are you?"

"They want fifty G's for his safe return," Benny said.

"Don't tell me, don't tell me," The Silver Fox said, covering his ears.

"I tried to buy some phony bills, but . . ."

"Don't tell me!"

A knock sounded on the door.

"Thank God," The Silver Fox said, and hurried to answer it. Benny sat morosely at the long table covered with stolen silver, listening to the voices in the entrance foyer. He did not think it would be safe to keep the second fifty thousand dollars, as his friend Silvio had advised. Maybe nobody likes to be reminded of his mistakes, but when somebody's involved who's *already* made a mistake, the person making the *second* mistake might think he had an edge in asking the person who made the *first* mistake to *correct* the second mistake, or so Benny reasoned. Besides, keeping the fifty thousand had never crossed his mind. Well, it had crossed it. But only fleetingly. *Those that much covet are with gain so fond, for what they have not, that which they possess they scatter and unloose it from their bond, and so, by hoping more, they have but less,* Benny quoted silently, and sighed. The only thing that had actually *lingered* in his mind was the idea of using the second fifty thousand to ransom Ganooch's son. Then, if Mario Azzecca *did* come to him and say, "Hey, Benny Napkins, where's that second fifty thousand dollars?" Benny could answer, "I used it to ransom Ganooch's son," which was a worthy cause.

"Do you know Dominick the Guru?" The Silver Fox asked.

Benny turned and looked at the young man standing in the doorway to the living room. "Yes, I believe we've met," he said, "but that was before you had the beard and the long hair."

"How do you like it this way?" Dominick said, walking over and shaking hands.

"It's becoming," Benny said.

"It's becoming too long," The Silver Fox said, wagging his head. "Nice Italian boy."

"Bloomingdales doesn't like it neither," Dominick said. "By the way," he added, turning to The Silver Fox, "he said to tell you he hopes you get hit by a subway."

"Why?" The Silver Fox asked. "Because his sister's a no-good whore? Whereas everybody knows that anyway?"

"I'm merely conveying his regards," Dominick said. *Boy, what bullshit,* he thought.

"What have you brought me?" The Silver Fox asked. He noticed Dominick's sidelong glance and quickly said, "You can trust Benny. He's an old friend."

Dominick studied him for a moment, and then went out into the foyer again.

"What shall I do?" Benny whispered to The Silver Fox.

"About what?"

"About Ganooch's son?"

"I never heard nothing about Ganooch's son."

"I just told you . . ."

"I don't even know if he has a son or not. *Has* he got a son? Never mind, don't tell me."

Dominick came back into the room, carrying a suitcase which he hoisted onto the long wooden table. "Lots of nice stuff here," he said, and opened the bag. The Silver Fox picked up a magnifying glass, and began examining the pieces.

"Did you see this?" Dominick asked Benny.

"What is it?" Benny asked.

"A wrist watch," Dominick said, and handed it to him.

"Very nice," Benny said, and looked at it distractedly.

"Who's that whose picture's on the watch?" The Silver Fox asked.

"That's the Vice-President," Dominick said.

"Herbert Humphrey? It don't even look like him," The Silver Fox said.

Benny was about to return the watch to Dominick when, for no reason whatever, for no good reason that he could think of, he turned it over and looked at the back. There was an inscription on the case. The inscription read:

"Where did you get this watch!" Benny shouted.

*   *   *

In a blue Plymouth sedan borrowed from his old friend Arthur Doppio, Snitch drove up to Larchmont that afternoon to pay a visit to the Ganucci governess. He had been promised twenty-five dollars if he could come up with information Bozzaris did not already possess, and Snitch was not a man to let twenty-five dollars slip away quite that easily. He drove up the long tree-lined driveway to Many Maples, parked the car in the oval before the sumptuous front entrance, walked onto the flagstone portico, admired the brass escutcheon with the single word *Ganucci* inscribed upon it, and then rang the bell and waited.

Nanny opened the door immediately, almost as if she had been standing behind it and waiting for expected company. When she saw Snitch, her face fell.

"Yes?" she said.

"Nanny," Snitch said, "I think I have some further information about that felony you say was committed Tuesday night."

"Yes?" she said.

"Yes. Would it be all right if I came in? You never know who's hiding in the bushes these days."

"Come in," she said, and because it was exactly two P.M., the clocks in the living room all tolled the hour, *Bong, Bong,* and were finished almost before they began. Snitch looked at his wrist watch.

"Three minutes slow," he said, and followed Nanny into the study. "Very nice place Ganooch has here," he remarked.

"Yes," Nanny said. "What information have you got for me?"

"I know there's fifty thousand dollars involved," Snitch said, referring to the cable he had seen on Mario Azzecca's desk. Judging from the way Nanny went suddenly pale, he suspected he had struck pay dirt.

Her hand went to her throat. In a tiny, quiet voice, she said, "Yes, that's right."

"'Essential and urgent raise fifty delivery Saturday,'" Snitch said, narrowing his eyes as he quoted exactly from the cable now, figuring what the hell.

"Is that what the last note meant?" Nanny asked.

"Precisely," Snitch said. He recognized that he had seen only one note (which, in fact, had been a cable rather than a note), and that he hadn't the faintest notion whether it had been the first note, the last note, or the one in between. But he felt he had gained Nanny's confidence, and if he could continue to sustain her belief in knowledge he did not truly possess, he might eventually get the information Bozzaris wanted. Besides, intrigue was the most exciting profession in the world.

"Saturday when?" Nanny asked.

"Don't *you* know?"

"No," she said. "I couldn't make heads nor tails of the last note. Benny couldn't either. I read it to him on the phone."

"Benny?"

"Napkins."

"Oh yes. He knows about this, huh?"

"Yes. I rang him up the moment I knew he was gone."

"I see," Snitch said, not knowing what she was talking about.

"Where did *you* see the note?" Nanny asked.

"On Mario Azzecca's desk."

"Mario . . . oh my!" she said, and put her hand to her throat again. "Does *he* know about it too?"

"Sure he does. It was addressed to him," Snitch said.

"Addressed to Mario Azzecca? But why?"

"I guess because when Ganooch wants fifty thousand dollars, he drops a little note to his lawyer and tells him to get it for him. That's why."

"Ganooch?"

"Sure."

"Mr. *Ganucci* asked Mario Azzecca for fifty thousand dollars?"

"Sure," Snitch said, and shrugged.

Nanny looked as if she were about to faint. She leaned back against the bookcases and almost dislodged *The Rubáiyát* from its shelf. When she spoke again, her voice was a whisper. "He knows," she said, her eyes wide.

"Knows what?" Snitch said.

"All about it," Nanny said. "Oh my God, he knows all about it." She put her hand on Snitch's arm. "He'll kill us. Both of us. Me, and Benny as well." Her hand tightened. "Do you know who has him?" she asked.

"Benny? Jeanette Kay, ain't it? He's got an arrangement with Jeanette Kay, ain't he?"

"No, the boy."

"Benny's living with a *boy*?"

"I mean, do you know who the *kidnapers* are?" she said impatiently.

"What?" Snitch said.

"The kidnapers."

"What?" he said again.

She was standing directly in front of him now, peering up into his eyes. "Snitch, do you know who kidnaped Mr. Ganucci's son?" she asked, and Snitch thought, *So that's it, huh? That's some felony, all right, that's as big as they come.* He needed time to think. There was money to be made out of this situation, if only he could figure out how. A little time was all he needed, but a little time was the one thing Nanny seemed unwilling to grant. Her hand clutched tightly onto his arm, her eyes blazing up into his, she insistently demanded once again, "Do-you-know-who-kidnaped-Lewis-Ganucci?"

"Yes," Snitch said, figuring what the hell.

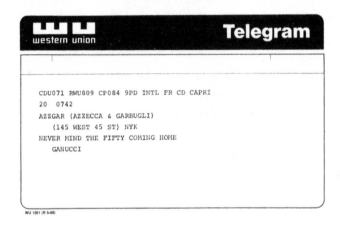

```
western union                    Telegram

    CDU071 RWU809 CP084 9PD INTL FR CD CAPRI
    20  0742
    AZZGAR (AZZECCA & GARBUGLI)
       (145 WEST 45 ST) NYK
    NEVER MIND THE FIFTY COMING HOME
       GANUCCI
```
WU 1201 (R 5-69)

"Seven words," Garbugli said. "A goddamn masterpiece."

"Yes, but what do we do now?" Azzecca wanted to know.

"We call Benny Napkins and get the money back."

"Right," Azzecca said, and went immediately to the telephone. He dialed Benny's number, waited, and then heard a sleepy voice say, "Hello?"

"Hello, who's this?" Azzecca asked.

"Jeanette Kay. Who's this?"

"Mario Azzecca."

"Hello, Mr. Azzecca, how are you?" Jeanette Kay said.

"Fine. Is Benny there?"

"No, he's not."

"Where is he?"

"I don't know. I was sleeping when he left."

"He didn't go to the airport, did he?"

"I don't think so. Why would he go to the airport?"

"Tell him to call me the minute he gets in. And tell him *not* to go to Naples."

"Why would he go to Naples?" Jeanette Kay asked.

"Just tell him," Azzecca said, and hung up. "He's not home," he said to Garbugli. "You don't think he left for the airport already, do you?"

"At three o'clock?" Garbugli said. "His plane doesn't leave till ten tonight."

"Lots of people like to get to the airport early," Azzecca said. "It relieves anxiety symptoms."

"Let's call Nonaka and put him on the prowl."

"Nonaka? Why him?"

"In case Benny has any thoughts about maybe not returning that money."

"Even so. Nonaka."

"Best man for the job, Counselor."

"Nonaka gives me the shivers," Azzecca said.

"Call him," Garbugli said.

Azzecca shrugged and went to the telephone. He opened the address pad on his desk, searched through the Ns, and dialed Nonaka's number.

"Hello?" a voice on the other end whispered.

"Let me speak to Nonaka," Azzecca said.

"He's not here," the voice whispered.

"Where is he?"

"I don't know."

"Can't you talk a little louder?" Azzecca said, annoyed.

"Yes, but thank God, I don't have to," the voice whispered, and hung up.

"He's not home," Azzecca said.

"Who's that?" Luther Patterson asked his wife. He was standing at the window in the master bedroom, staring down at the backyard ten stories below. Ida came up beside him and looked.

"Where?" she said.

"There," he said. "Those three men. Who are those three men?"

"I don't see anybody," she said.

"Near the telephone pole there. Those three men. The seedy-looking one, and the one with the beard, and the Chinaman."

"Maybe they're telephone repairmen," Ida said.

"Have you ever seen a Chinese telephone repairman?" Luther asked.

"How can you tell he's Chinese?"

"I can see him, can't I?"

"From way up here?"

"My eyes are very good when I have my glasses on," Luther said. "He's Chinese." A sudden thought occurred to him. "What did Simon say?" he asked. "Something. Something about the Chinese, or China. Something." He rushed into the living room and pulled the *Collected Works* from his bookshelf. Rapidly turning pages, he came upon the review he'd been searching for. Aloud, he read:

His style is sheer chinoiserie, piling lacquered screens of paradox upon pagodas of hyperbole—sometimes a trifle schematically, but with unquenchable verve, bravado, and iconoclastic bravura.

Luther bowed his head in admiration.

"Stunning," he whispered in awe. "Positively stunning. Look to your laurels, Mr. Updike, there's another formidable John upon the scene."

Ida came into the room. Hands on hips, she said, "What does Simon say? Is he Chinese?"

"He doesn't comment," Luther answered. "But I know a Chinaman when I see one."

15: NONAKA

Tamaichi Nonaka Japanese.

He stood in the backyard with Benny Napkins on his left and Dominick the Guru on his right, and together they stared up at the sun-blinded windows on the rear of the building.

"It's hard to say," Dominick said. "I was in a lot of apartments last night."

"The only one we're concerned with is the one where you picked up that watch," Benny said.

"Yeah, yeah, I know. But it's hard to tell one window from another window, you know what I mean? I mean, all windows look the same to me. You go in them, you come out of them, they all look the same."

"*Try* to remember," Benny said. "Somewhere in that goddamn building is Carmine Ganucci's kid. If we can bust in and get the kid back we'll all be heroes. If not . . ."

"Listen, how did *I* get involved in this?" Dominick asked. "I was minding my own business, trying to engage in a simple act of commerce with The Silver Fox. Now all at once I'm involved in a kidnapping."

"Me too," Nonaka said.

"*You* are involved because *I* am involved," Benny said. "*No man is an Iland, intire of itselfe,*" he went on. "*Every man is a peece of the Continent, a part of the maine; if a Clod bee washed away by the Sea, Europe is the lesse, as well as if a Promontorie were, as well as if a Mannor of thy friends or of thine owne were; any man's death diminishes me, because I am involved in Mankinde; and therefore never send to know for whom the bell tolls; it tolls for thee.*"

"I never thought of it that way," Dominick said.

"Me too," Nonaka said.

"And besides, Ganooch will bust our heads if he ever finds out we knew which building his son was in, and couldn't remember the apartment."

"Maybe it was on the eighth floor," Dominick said, and shrugged.

"Maybe is not good enough," Benny said. "*Was* it the eighth floor, or was it not? I don't intend to go breaking down a door and suddenly find out there's a little old lady inside whose husband is a cop."

"Hey, there *was* a lady inside," Dominick said. "In fact, the kid called her by name."

"What did he call her?"

"Iris? Irene? Something like that. Something beginning with an I."

"Ina?" Benny asked.

"No."

"Ilka?" Nonaka asked.

"No."

"Ingrid?"

"No."

"Irma?"

"No."

"Isabel?"

"No, no."

"Inez."

"No."

"Isadora?"

"No."

"I can't think of any other names beginning with an I," Benny said. "Would you recognize the apartment if you saw it again?"

"Maybe."

"What I'm trying to say is, if you went up the fire escape there and looked in the windows, would one of the rooms seem familiar to you?"

"Maybe. But I'm not about to go up that fire escape in broad daylight."

"What time is it now?" Benny asked.

"A little after three."

"It won't be dark till maybe eight, eight-thirty," Benny said.

"So what's the hurry?" Dominick asked.

"What's the *hurry*? Suppose they *kill* that little kid?"

"Nobody would do a crazy thing like that," Dominick said.

"*I* would," Nonaka said, making conversation.

He was not, of course, referring to Carmine Ganucci's son, though if Ganooch asked even *that* little favor of him, Nonaka might have been willing to comply. The thing that motivated Nonaka was that he had been 4-F during World War II (because of a slight hernia) and had never been drafted to fight. Carmine Ganucci, in Nonaka's mind, was carrying on the noble tradition of battling the Fascist Pigs. Not that Nonaka liked breaking heads so much. What he liked most was breaking doors with his bare hands. That was what really thrilled him. He liked to bring back his arm, bent at the elbow, and then release it like a piston, the hand held stiff and rigid, and he liked to yell, "Hrrrraaaaagh!" and hit the door with the hard edge of his hand, and watch it splinter. Boy, he really liked to do that. He was disappointed that he would have to wait till it got dark to hit a door. But of course, Benny Napkins was right; you couldn't go smashing down doors unless you knew what was on the other side of them.

Once, when Nonaka had been a much younger man, he had gone out to Hicksville (Long Island) on a job for Ganucci and had broken an aluminum screen door with one swipe of his hand, and then had given a chop at the inside wooden door, almost shattering the jamb in the bargain, and then had run into the living room, heading for the back bedroom of the small development house, where he hoped to break down yet another door. What he found on the floor of the living room was three people with bullet holes in their heads. That was when he heard a police siren coming from the vicinity of Old Country Road, and decided he had better get out of there fast because somebody had beaten him to the punch.

It was later discovered that Ganucci had got his wires crossed somehow, sending Nonaka to Hicksville instead of to Syosset, and sending the other fellows to do the job Nonaka was supposed to do. As a result, a very fancy deadbeat named Oscar the Pimp got away to Jamaica (Long Island) and had to be sought for thirty days and thirty nights before he was found living off the proceeds with a girl named Alice. It was Nonaka who finally located Oscar in the Jamaica rooming house, and therefore had the opportunity to break down first the door to the room, and then the door to the bathroom, where he found Oscar taking a bath in the same tub with Alice. Oscar later drowned.

"What do you want to do, Benny?" Dominick asked.

"Let's go get a drink someplace, and wait till it gets dark."

"I could use a drink," Dominick said.

"Me too," Nonaka said.

*   *   *

Carmine Ganucci had boarded a plane from Naples at 2:40 P.M. local time and had arrived at London's Heathrow Airport at 5:05 P.M. local time, where he had transferred to another plane that left England at 6:15 P.M. local time. Because of the vagaries of date lines and daylight saving time and such, he had already been over the Atlantic Ocean for several hours by the time Snitch got back to the city. In fact, Ganucci's plane was scheduled to land at Kennedy at 9:05 P.M., exactly six hours from the moment Snitch parked Arthur Doppio's car in a space on Second Avenue and walked up the street to the tenement where Arthur lived with two cats and a myna bird. The bird had a vast vocabulary, knew far more Italian than Arthur did, and was often heard to shout, *"Lasciate ogni speranza, voi ch'entrate!"* over the roar of the beer drinkers sometimes found in Arthur's apartment.

Snitch did not know that Carmine Ganucci was airborne, otherwise he might have reconsidered. As it was, he found Arthur teaching the myna bird a new word.

"Why are you teaching him that particular word?" Snitch asked.

"I think it's a good word for the bird to know," Arthur said.

"It's a word I never even heard of."

"I got it out of the dictionary," Arthur said.

"I never heard of it."

"Did you ever hear of vermouth cassis?" Arthur asked.

"Never. Though a lot of information comes my way," Snitch said.

"It's a drink. It's supposed to be delicious. Freddie Corriere was with a young lady last night who drank nothing but vermouth cassis. She said it was delicious. In fact, Freddie told me . . ."

"I don't wish to interrupt," Snitch said, "but how would you like to pick up some change doing nothing at all?"

"What would I have to do?" Arthur asked.

"I just told you. Nothing at all. Does the idea appeal to you?"

"Of course it does."

"All you have to do is say you kidnaped Carmine Ganucci's kid," Snitch said.

"You're crazy," Arthur said. "I like you a lot, Snitch, but you're crazy. Listen, would you like to hear what Freddie and this girl done last night? He met her in this bar, you see . . ."

"What we'll do," Snitch said, "is we'll tell Nanny you're the guy who . . ."

"Who's Nanny?"

"The Ganucci governess."

"Oh yeah, the one he brought over from London, England, right?"

"Right."

"What about her?"

"We'll tell her you snatched the Ganucci kid . . ."

"I don't want . . ."

". . . and that you'll bring him back as soon as she gives you the ransom money. How does that sound to you?"

"Terrible. I don't want to be nowhere near nothing that smells of snatching Ganooch's kid. Snitch, I like you a lot, I really do, but you're a little crazy, I mean it."

"You could wear a mask," Snitch said.

"I don't have a mask," Arthur said.

"You could pull a nylon stocking over your head."

"I don't have no nylon stockings."

"I know where we can get one," Snitch said. "The Jackass has a whole drawer full of nylon stockings."

"Then get *him* to help you."

"He's too stupid," Snitch said. "This job requires somebody with brains."

"Me?" Arthur said.

"Right," Snitch said.

"How much money is involved here?"

"Fifty thousand."

"That's a lot of money."

"Let's say we *could* get ahold of a nylon stocking someplace," Snitch said. "Then you could sit down and talk to Nanny with the stocking pulled over your head. And tell her to hand over the money. And promise to bring the kid back."

"How do I do that?" Arthur said.

"Do what?"

"Bring the kid back. Where *is* the kid?"

"I don't know."

"Then how can I bring him back?"

"That's *her* problem, ain't it?"

"It's also *my* problem if Ganooch finds out I took fifty G's from the little lady he's got living there in his house."

"How could Ganooch find out? And how could anybody know it's you if you got a stocking pulled over your head?"

Arthur thought this over for a few moments.

"Why not?" he said at last.

"Why not?" Snitch said.

"Intercourse," the myna bird said.

It was strange how something could be sitting there right under a person's nose, and a person could never notice it. Take Marie Pupattola.

"Take a letter, Marie," Azzecca said.

"Yes, Mr. Azzecca," she answered.

She was sitting in a chair opposite his desk, her long legs crossed, her red hair burnished by the late afternoon sun that streamed through the windows. She was wearing a very short skirt which she occasionally tugged at but which for the most part she seemed content to leave exactly where it was, allowing

Azzecca the opportunity to look clear up to her behind. It was strange how he had never noticed before.

"How long have you been working here?" Azzecca said.

"Is this the letter?" Marie asked.

"No, it's a question."

"I've been working here for seventeen months, Mr. Azzecca. Didn't you know that?"

"I knew it was more than a year, but I didn't know it was seventeen months."

"Yes," Marie said, and tugged at her skirt.

"You are a very pretty girl, Marie."

"Why thank you, Mr. Azzecca," Marie said.

"Why don't you come sit on my lap?" Azzecca said.

"Why, Mr. Azzecca!" Marie said in surprise.

"It would be more comfortable than your chair," Azzecca said, "and also I wouldn't have to shout while dictating."

"My chair is very comfortable," Marie said, "and also I can hear you fine, Mr. Azzecca."

"Don't you like me?" Azzecca asked.

"You are a wonderful employer, Mr. Azzecca," Marie said.

"Then why won't you come sit on my lap?"

"Oh well," Marie said, and shrugged.

"You are a very pretty girl, Marie, did I tell you that?"

"Yes, Mr. Azzecca. You told me that a few minutes ago."

"It's funny that I never noticed it until yesterday afternoon when you were lying about Snitch having seen that cable."

"I wasn't lying, Mr. Azzecca."

"You were lying, Marie, and lying is a serious thing. I know people who have actually been *fired* for lying about something that was terribly serious and important to their employers."

"Oh, but I wasn't lying. Mr. Delatore *was* sound asleep when I put the cable on your desk. I swear to God."

"Don't take the name of the Lord in vain, Marie," Azzecca said.

"Well, it's true," she said, and shrugged again.

"Come sit on my lap, Marie."

"Well, why don't you just give me the letter?" Marie suggested.

"Marie, I am going to tell you something. Do you know, Marie, that I have been married for twenty-seven years to the same woman?"

"I didn't know that, Mr. Azzecca."

"It's the truth. Twenty-seven years. I have been married to an Irish girl for twenty-seven years. Sybil. She's Irish. Sybil Brogan was her maiden name. Do you know what my father, may he rest in peace, said to me when I told him I was going to marry an Irish girl?"

"What did he say, Mr. Azzecca?"

"He said, 'You're going to marry a *what*?'"

"What did you say?"

"I said, 'An Irish girl.'"

"What did he say?"

"He didn't say anything. He stuck his head in the oven." Azzecca smiled. "That's a little joke, Marie. He didn't really stick his head in the oven. I was making a little joke."

"Oh," Marie said.

"What my father really said was, 'Listen, Mario, it's your funeral.'"

"What a terrible thing to say!" Marie said.

"Terrible," Azzecca said. "Do you want to know something?"

"What?"

"He was right."

"Oh, Mr. Azzecca!" Marie said.

"Marie, he was right. What's right is right, my father was right. Twenty-seven years to the same woman, and do you know what I've got? I've got an eight-by-ten study in a twelve-room apartment. Would you believe that, Marie?"

"Oh, that's terrible, Mr. Azzecca," Marie said.

"Is it terrible? It *is* terrible, isn't it? Do you know what my main pleasure in life is, Marie?"

"What, Mr. Azzecca?"

"Looking at the Delacorte fountain."

"Oh, please, Mr. Azzecca, you'll make me cry."

"I'm just a person, Marie, like anyone else. A human being who craves affection every now and then. Don't we all, Marie? Tell the truth."

"Oh *yes,* Mr. Azzecca."

"So come here and sit on my lap."

"I don't think I could, Mr. Azzecca."

"You could, you could. Give it a try."

"No, I don't think so," Marie said, and shook her head, and uncrossed her legs, and then crossed them again, and tugged at her skirt. "Why don't you just give me the letter, Mr. Azzecca? I think that would be best all around."

"I know what you're thinking, Marie. You're thinking it would be wrong, am I right?"

"Right, right."

"You're a nice Italian girl, a Catholic, you're probably still a virgin . . ."

"Yes, probably."

". . . and you're thinking why should you start up with a man who's been married to the same Irish woman for twenty-seven years, that's what you're probably thinking. You're thinking it would be wrong."

"That's right, Mr. Azzecca."

"Why would it be wrong, Marie?"

"It just would," Marie said, and shrugged.

"Marie, it would be beautiful. Marie, there are arrangements all over this city, all over the *world,* Marie. Lonely people make arrangements with each other, Marie, because they *need* each other. Did you ever read a book called *The Arrangement,* Marie?"

"No, I don't think so."

"It was a fine book, Marie. It was all about arrangements. I would like to make an arrangement with you, Marie."

"Gee, Mr. Azzecca, thank you, but I think maybe you'd better give me the letter because it's getting late, you know, and I have a lot of other things on my desk."

"Marie, I could name people who have arrangements that you would never dream had arrangements."

"Who?" Marie said, and leaned forward, and did not tug at her skirt.

"Benny Napkins has an arrangement with Jeanette Kay Pezza."

"Yes, I know that."

"Paulie Secondo has an arrangement with a German airline stewardess from Düsseldorf."

"Düsseldorf!" Marie said.

"Snitch Delatore's former wife has an arrangement with a Pokerino barker from Amarillo, Texas."

"Amarillo, Texas!" Marie said.

"Even Carmine Ganucci has an arrangement," Azzecca said, lowering his voice.

"Carmine Ganucci!"

"An arrangement, yes," Azzecca whispered. "With a very pretty little thing who used to be a high-priced hooker. The things I could tell you about arrangements, Marie."

"*Don't* tell me, Mr. Azzecca. I don't want to know."

"Come sit on my lap, Marie."

"I would, Mr. Azzecca. Believe me, I would. There's only one trouble."

"Are you afraid?"

"No."

"Are you reluctant to start an arrangement with someone who is also your employer?"

"Oh no, it isn't that. In fact . . ."

"Yes, Marie?"

"I already *have* an arrangement, you see. With someone who *is* also my employer. With Vito, you see. With Mr. Garbugli. With your partner."

"I see," Azzecca said.

"Yes," Marie said.

"Take a letter," Azzecca said.

"Hello, Nanny?" Snitch said.

"Yes?"

"This is Snitch."

"Yes, Snitch?"

"I have made contact with the certain party we were discussing earlier today."

"Yes."

"He is willing to conclude negotiations with you, provided he may remain incognito."

"Granted," Nanny said.

"Also, he would like the money tonight."

"What time tonight?"

"I thought he could drive to Larchmont as soon as it gets dark. He is wearing a nylon stocking over his head, you see, and he don't want to attract no attention from passer-bys."

"I understand. What time will he get here?"

"Eight, eight-thirty. Will you have the money by then?"

"I have the money already," Nanny said.

"Fine. Then there's no problem," Snitch said.

"None whatever. I shall look forward to seeing your friend later tonight."

"Nanny, he ain't no friend of mine," Snitch said. "Please remember that. If this ever should come to Ganooch's attention, I want it understood that I'm only doing this out of respect for him. I never saw this guy before in my life, and as I told you he'll be wearing a stocking over his face, so I never *will* get to know who he is."

"I understand."

"There's nothing in this for me, Nanny. I'm just doing a favor for a man I happen to love and admire, Carmine Ganucci."

"I'm sure Mr. Ganucci will one day express his appreciation," Nanny said. "In any event, I'll be waiting for your friend's arrival."

"Eight, eight-thirty," Snitch said.

"Is the boy safe?" Nanny asked.

"Well, would you like to talk to this certain party himself? He's right here with me."

"Yes, I would."

"He's wearing his stocking right this minute," Snitch said, "so he may be a little difficult to understand."

"Put him on," Nanny said.

"Hello?" the voice said.

"Is this the certain party to whom we were referring earlier?" Nanny asked.

"Right," the voice said.

"As I understand it, you'll be here at eight, eight-thirty."

"Right."

"Is the boy safe?"

"Yes."

"Will he be returned as soon as we complete our negotiations?"

"Yes."

"Then I take it you will have him with you?"

"Right."

"Hello, Nanny," Snitch said. "I couldn't help overhearing what you just asked. You understand, don't you, that for this certain party's protection, he'll probably leave the kid where he is now, until all the business transaction is taken care of. For his own protection, I mean, though I agree with you he's the scum of the earth."

"I understand," Nanny said.

"Good. Well, *hasta la vista*," Snitch said, and hung up.

Nonaka was getting very drunk. No one at the table seemed to notice it because they were all getting very drunk too. The bar was on Ninety-sixth Street and Columbus Avenue, and it was called The Homestead. On the plate-glass window that faced the street, Nonaka read the name of the bar as deatsemoH ehT, which sounded very Japanese to him. Everything sounded very Japanese to him right now. Even Benny Napkins sounded Japanese.

"The dilemma here is a moral dilemma," Benny said. "That's the way I see it."

"How do you see it?" Dominick said. "Let's have another drink."

"Okay," Benny said. "Bartender," he said, and raised his hand.

"Japanese people can't say the letter 'l.' Did you know that?" Nonaka said.

"What do you mean?"

"Like dilemma," Nonaka said. "Japanese people can't say the word dilemma because there's an 'l' in it."

"I didn't know that," Benny said.

"Name your poison," the bartender said.

"Another round," Benny said.

"You guys are getting plastered," the bartender said.

"There's another one," Nonaka said. "Plastered. Impossible for a Japanese to say plastered. Or even polluted."

"You guys are getting both plastered *and* polluted," the bartender said, and walked away.

"The reason it's a dilemma is that it has twin forks. It's a twin-forked dilemma," Benny said.

"What are the two forks?" Dominick asked.

"*Twin* forks," Benny said, "*twin* forks. Fifty thousand dollars a fork. Twins."

"Dollars, there's another one," Nonaka said.

"Do you know how much money I have in my possession?" Benny asked.

"How much?" Dominick said.

"A hundred thousand dollars," Benny said.

"Dollars," Nonaka said, shaking his head. "Impossible to say.

"That's a lot of money," Dominick said. "Do you know the most money I ever seen in my life?"

"What?" Benny said.

"In a single bill, I mean?"

"Bill, there's another one."

"How much?"

"A thousand dollars," Dominick said. "Do you know who's on the thousand-dollar bill?"

"Who?" Benny said.

"Grover Cleveland."

"Cleveland, impossible," Nonaka said. "The whole language is full of l's."

"You know who *used* to be on the thousand-dollar bill?"

"Who?"

"Alexander Hamilton."

"Do you know how a Japanese would say Alexander Hamilton?" Nonaka asked.

"How?"

"Arexander Hamirton." He blinked his eyes.

"Why would he say that?" Dominick asked.

"I don't know," Nonaka said, and shrugged.

"Well, we all have our little problems," Dominick said.

"Look at all the goddamn l's," Nonaka said.

Benny looked, but he didn't see anything. Besides, he had his own little problem. His problem was a simple one: if they didn't find the kid someplace in that building, what should he do? Should he give Nanny one of the fifty-thousand-dollar bundles and take the other one to Naples as instructed? Or should he keep one of the fifty-thousand-dollar bundles for himself and the hell with Ganucci, the hell with everybody, just grab Jeanette Kay Pezza and take her to Honolulu and lay on the sand with his head on her nice big tits? The problem with life was that it was full of problems, especially if a hundred thousand dollars was burning a hole in your pocket.

"Boy," he said.

"You said it," Dominick said.

"Me too," Nonaka said.

The bartender brought another round. The men sat drinking silently. Through the plate-glass window, Benny could see men in business suits coming out of the subway kiosk to wend their way homeward in the early evening hours, home to wife and loved ones, home to cooking smells, home to a weekend of fun and frivolity after five long days of hard work in offices hither and yon throughout Manhattan. For an insane but fleeting instant, Benny almost wished he was an honest citizen.

At seven o'clock that evening, Luther Patterson dialed Many Maples and asked to talk to Carmine Ganucci.

"Mr. Ganucci is not at home," Nanny said. "He is in Italy."

"Oh, the old Italy gag again, huh?" Luther said.

"Who *is* this?" Nanny asked.

"The kidnaper," Luther said.

"This is not the kidnaper," Nanny said.

"Are *you* trying to tell *me* what I am?" Luther said. "Madam . . ."

"I spoke to the kidnaper not two hours ago," Nanny said.

"How could you have spoken to me two hours ago, when two hours ago I was sitting here . . . ?"

"I was put in touch with the kidnaper two hours ago. A trusted friend put me in touch with the kidnaper. I have already arranged a meeting with him. I don't know who *this* is . . ."

"*This* is the goddamn *kidnaper!*" Luther shouted frantically.

"No," Nanny said.

"Madam, that other man is a fraud! Whoever's representing himself to you as the kidnaper . . ."

"Good day, sir," Nanny said, and hung up.

Luther looked at the mouthpiece. Angrily, he dialed the Larchmont number again, and waited until the phone rang on the other end.

"Many Maples," Nanny said.

"Madam, I warn you . . ."

"If you don't stop bothering me," Nanny said, "I will notify the police."

"Madam, you are playing a very dangerous game here. The life of an innocent child . . ."

There was a click on the line.

Luther replaced the receiver on its cradle. He rose from his desk and began pacing the room. He went back to the phone, lifted the receiver, put it back on its cradle again, lifted it yet another time, and then slammed it down viciously.

"What the hell is going on?" he shouted.

"Did you say something?" Ida called from the kitchen.

"Get that boy in here!" Luther shouted.

16: LITTLE LEWIS

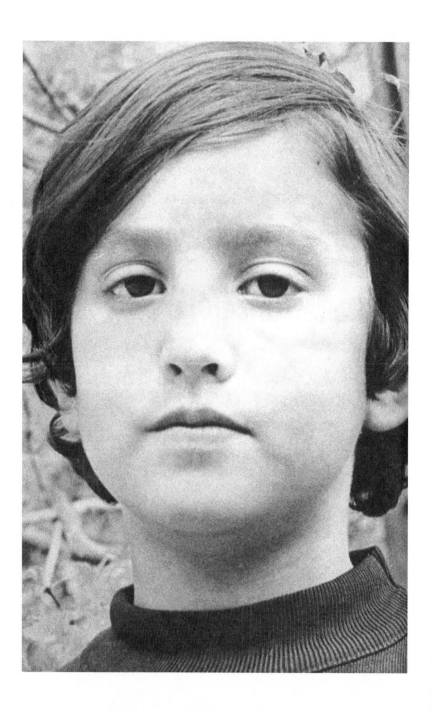

Luther pointed to a wing chair alongside the inoperative fireplace and said, "Sit."

Lewis climbed into the chair, folded his hands in his lap, and looked across the room to where Luther peered at him from behind his desk. Ida stood in the doorway, drying her hands on her apron. Luther kept staring at the boy. In the kitchen, an electric clock hummed discreetly.

"My watch is missing," Lewis said.

"Never mind your watch, I want to ask you some questions," Luther said.

"It was on the dresser," Lewis said.

"I said never mind the watch," Luther said. "Let's talk about your father."

"He's the one who *gave* me the watch," Lewis said. "For my birthday."

"I don't care what he gave you," Luther said. "I want to know where he is now."

"Who?"

"Your father."

"In Italy."

"Then it's true," Luther said, and rolled his eyes toward the ceiling. "John, it's really true. He's in Italy."

"Who's John?" Lewis asked, looking up at the ceiling.

"Where in Italy?" Luther asked.

"Capri."

"It's true," Luther mumbled. "Oh, God, it's true."

"Do you have a cleaning lady?" Lewis asked.

"What?"

"Because maybe *she* stole the watch."

"Nobody stole your damn watch. Who's in charge there?"

"Where?"

"In Larchmont. At your house. At Many Maples. While your father's away."

"Nanny."

"Does she know your voice?"

"Sure. My voice? Sure, she does."

"I want you to talk to her on the telephone."

"What for?"

"Because she won't believe me. I want you to talk to her, and tell her you're alive and well, and that she'd better get the money right away because we're not kidding around here. Do you understand me?"

"What money?" Lewis asked.

"The money to guarantee your safe return."

"What if she *doesn't* get the money?" Ida asked suddenly.

"She'll get it, don't worry," Luther said.

"Answer me, Luther."

"I *have* answered you."

"You're not planning on hurting him, are you?"

"I am planning on getting the money," Luther said.

"Because if you touch him . . ."

"Please be quiet, Ida."

"If you lay a hand on him . . ."

"Quiet, quiet."

"I'll kill you," Ida said gently.

"Very nice," Luther said. He looked toward the ceiling. "Nice talk for a wife, eh, Martin? Very nice talk."

"I mean it," Ida said.

"Nobody's going to kill anybody," Luther said. "We're . . ."

"My *father* might," Lewis said. "He knows a lot of tough guys."

"Your father does not know any tough guys," Luther said.

"Oh yes, he does."

"Oh no, he does not. When I was your age, I thought *my* father knew a lot of tough guys, too, but he *didn't.* They were merely his normal drinking companions. They only *seemed* tough because I was a bright, sensitive child who . . ."

"Well, these guys *are* tough," Lewis protested. "I saw them."

"I do not wish to waste any more time discussing fantasy as opposed to objective reality, do you understand?" Luther said.

"No."

"I'm going to call your house now . . ."

"They *are* tough. They have guns and everything."

"Um-huh," Luther said, "guns and everything." He went to the telephone. "When I get your governess on the line, I want you to come here immediately and talk to her."

Lewis, offended, would not answer.

"Do you hear me?"

Sulking, Lewis nodded briefly.

"Good," Luther said, and began dialing.

"Even the policemen were a little scared," Lewis said.

"Mm-huh," Luther said, and waited while the phone began ringing in Larchmont.

"When they came to the house," Lewis said. "The policemen. Last year."

"Yes, yes," Luther said, and tapped his fingers impatiently on the desk.

"*All* my father's friends were there," Lewis said,

"With their guns, no doubt," Luther said.

"Yes, with their *guns*. And if you don't believe me, it was in the *Daily News*."

"Many Maples," Nanny's voice said on the other end of the line.

Luther's mouth fell open. His eyes wide behind his glasses, he stared speechlessly at the boy across the room, whose last words—coupled with what his governess had just said into the telephone—now triggered belated recognition. *Oh my God,* Luther thought, *oh my God.*

"Many Maples," Nanny said again, as though diabolically reiterating the name, and forcing Luther to recall in startlingly vivid black-and-white the two headlines that had paraded across the top of two separate stories in two separate newspapers not eleven months ago. The first headline was printed in the bold type favored by the city's morning tabloid, and it read:

MAPLES MEET BUSTED

The second headline was printed in the more restrained type preferred by the city's *other* morning paper, and it read:

Gangland Summit Conference Raided

The headlines blinked alternately onto the screen of Luther's memory, burning themselves out at once, melting into molten type, then sinking to his heart, lodging there like a steaming cannon ball. *Many Maples,* he thought, *oh my God. Carmine Ganucci,* he thought, *oh my God.*

"Oh my God!" he moaned aloud, and instantly hung up. He bounded from his chair, clasped both hands to his head, looked at the ceiling, and shouted, "Don't either of you ever read the newspapers!"

"What is it?" Ida asked. "What's the matter?"

"We've got to take him home at once," Luther said. "My God, do you know whose son we've kidnaped?"

"Carmine Ganucci's," Lewis said.

17: ARTHUR

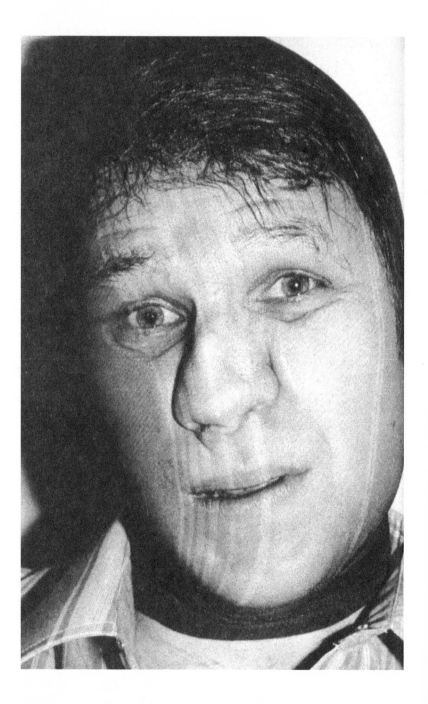

Ganucci had set his watch with New York time the moment they left the ground at Heathrow. It was now 7:50 P.M., which meant that in little more than an hour they would touch down at Kennedy. He glanced over at Stella, who was asleep in the seat beside him, snoring lightly. Good, he thought. He liked it when Stella went to sleep. It gave him time to consider his arrangement.

Ganucci always thought of himself as a sort of Cary Grant, and of his arrangement as a sort of Grace Kelly. Not that she looked at all like Grace Kelly, although he did resemble Cary Grant a lot, especially around the eyes. (He wished he could talk like Cary Grant, but what can you do?) In his mind, the way they had met had been almost like a movie. He could almost see the diatribe unfolding, just as if the lines were written in a screenplay and they were speaking them while looking into each other's eyes.

CARY: Excuse me for asking this, miss, but what is a nice
    girl like you doing in a place like this?
GRACE: What's wrong with this place?
CARY: It's a very nice place, but not for a girl like you.
GRACE: I think it's a very nice place.

CARY: So do I. Don't misunderstand me. You are the best lay I've had in this whole city. Maybe in the whole world.

GRACE: Then what are you complaining about?

CARY: Complaining? Who's complaining? Do I look like I'm complaining? I'm a very satisfied customer.

GRACE: Don't tell me, tell Madam Hortense.

CARY: I will, believe me. If you want me to. But I don't see why you should worry about her opinion, a girl like you with talent like you got, and class besides.

GRACE: I work for Madam Hortense.

CARY: That's exactly the point.

GRACE: I guess I'm missing the point.

CARY: I am thinking of a more permanent arrangement.

GRACE: This is a very permanent arrangement.

CARY: I was thinking you could leave here for an even more permanent arrangement.

GRACE: If I left here, Madam Hortense would break my head.

CARY: If you don't leave here, maybe *I* will break Madam Hortense's head, and yours besides.

GRACE: I never thought of it that way. What sort of an arrangement did you have in mind?

CARY: I had an arrangement in mind where you would leave here with me, and never come back. And where you wouldn't have to do what Madam Hortense tells you to do all the time. Only what I tell you to do.

GRACE: I fail to see the difference.

CARY: The difference is I am Carmine Ganucci.

GRACE: Oh.

Carmine Ganucci was getting an erection. He rang for the stewardess, and when she arrived, he asked her if she had any Alka-Seltzer. The stewardess spoke with an English accent, which didn't help at all. She asked him if he had a headache.

* * *

Benny Napkins was discovering that, unless a person is extremely sure-footed, a fire escape can be a difficult thing to negotiate even during the daytime; nighttime and darkness, not to mention intoxication, only compounded the difficulty. Nonaka did not help at all. Nonaka kept singing "Pretty Parasol and Fan" as they slowly staggered and stumbled their way up the narrow iron-runged ladders on the rear wall of the building. On the third floor, a lady poked her head out of a window, looked directly into Dominick the Guru's face, and said, "Oh!" Dominick replied, "Softball team, lady," grinned reassuringly, and continued up the ladder to the fourth floor. Behind him, Nonaka bowed to the lady, almost fell off the fire escape, regained his balance, and continued singing his little song. Benny kept wondering how many people in the city of New York fell off fire escapes as opposed to, say, bridges or tunnels.

Dominick was looking into yet another window.

"Recognize it?" Benny asked from below.

"Onward," Dominick said. "Upward."

"Who's that?" a man in his undershirt asked.

"Gas company," Dominick said.

"Is there a leak?"

"There's a leak," Dominick said.

"Good evening, sir," Nonaka said to the man, bowing.

"Good evening," the man answered, bewildered.

Nonaka went by singing.

"Where are your credentials?" the man asked Benny as he went past the window and started up the ladder to the next floor.

"In the car," Benny said over his shoulder.

"Oh. Okay," the man said, and pulled down his shade.

Snitch Delatore knew that fifty thousand dollars was a lot of money. Everybody knew that. Even Arthur Doppio knew that.

Snitch further knew that maybe, just maybe, there might possibly be a slender chance that Arthur could actually talk Nanny into parting with that kind of money tonight. But Snitch also knew, by heart, a proverb his sainted grandmother had taught him at her knee, *"Prendi i soldi e corri"*—which loosely translated into English as "Take the money and run." And whereas fifty thousand dollars was most assuredly the stuff on which dreams are made, there was a basic reality to twenty-five bucks in cold hard cash.

Everybody was in the money business, Snitch figured; it was merely a matter of how much a person was willing to settle for. His sainted grandmother would have settled for five dollars and a carton of name's day pastry. Given the intervening years and the rising spiral of inflation, Snitch felt that twenty-five dollars was only fair and reasonable recompense for a secret already shared by everybody and his brother, including Benny Napkins. Which is why he went to see Lieutenant Bozzaris, who had promised him *just* that sum for fresh and original information.

"Help you?" one of Bozzaris' fellows asked as Snitch stepped up to the gate in the slatted wood railing.

"I'd like to see the lieutenant," Snitch said.

"What about?"

"I have some information for him," Snitch said.

"Oh yeah, that's right," the detective said. "You're the stoolie."

Snitch made no reply. Sticks and stones could break his bones, but twenty-five bucks was twenty-five bucks. In silent dignity, he waited for the detective to check with Bozzaris. The door to the corner office opened at once, and Bozzaris himself stepped into the squadroom to greet him, hand extended.

"Well, well," Bozzaris said, "what a nice surprise!" he turned to the detective and yelled, "Sam! Two cups of coffee on the double!"

"We are out of coffee, Skipper!" Sam yelled back.

"See what I mean?" Bozzaris said. "There's never any coffee around here. What's the information you have for me, Snitch?"

"It's information about a major felony," Snitch said, and the telephone in Bozzaris' office began ringing.

On the tenth-floor fire escape, Dominick looked into yet another window, and said, "This is it."

"Are you sure?" Benny Napkins asked.

"Positive."

The three men crouched outside the window, peering into the bedroom. The sounds of the building seemed suddenly augmented, television sets blaring to the open-windowed night, toilets flushing, a woman laughing, someone practicing the piano, while far off on the street below, honking horns and grinding buses provided a staccato counterpoint. Nonaka listened nostalgically to the night music of the city and hummed again the song he'd learned at P.S. 80 on 120th Street, back when he'd been the only true American in a class of forty Wops.

They entered the apartment stealthily.

Dominick was the first to go in. He fell over the sill and knocked over a floor lamp.

"Shhh," Nonaka said behind him.

"Shhh," Benny said.

They picked Dominick up, righted the floor lamp, and waited silently while their eyes adjusted to the darkness.

"This is the room, all right," Dominick whispered. "There's the bed over there, and here's the dresser where I grabbed the watch."

"So where's the kid?" Benny whispered.

"I don't know," Dominick whispered.

Listening, they stood in the darkness.

"There's nobody here," Dominick said at last.

"How can you tell?"

"I'm an experienced burglar, I can tell. There's nobody here, the place is empty. Come on," Dominick said, and flicked on the lights.

Benny and Nonaka followed him into the corridor. The light from the open bedroom door illuminated a row of framed abstract prints, half a dozen in all, each in varying shades of blue and green that seemed to modulate into an oil painting hanging beside and beyond the last print, a huge gilt-framed canvas of an old lady drawing water from a well. Dominick, preceding them, threw another switch. An overhead light, covered with an imitation Tiffany shade, bathed the corridor in emerald-amber, tinting the old lady's face a deeper green and giving her a somewhat bilious look.

On the wall opposite the painting, there hung four framed photographs of men Benny had never seen or heard of, each gentleman identified by a small brass plaque set into the frame's molding, their respective and undoubtedly respected names engraved in discreet scroll: *Gilbert Millstein, Lester Goran, Richard P. Brickner,* and *Nat Freedland.* Over the entrance door to the next room, there was a pair of crossed Saracen swords that appeared to be razor-sharp. Dominick, like the village lamplighter, kept throwing switches, illuminating the way before them.

The room beyond the Saracen swords was a living room, or a library, it was difficult to tell which. Floor-to-ceiling bookcases lined one entire wall, running the length of the room to the windows at the far end. A desk stood before the windows, catching only a faint glow of light from West End Avenue, far below. Dominick turned on the desk lamp, throwing into bright illumination a pair of scissors, a paste-pot, a ream of white bond, a typewriter, and countless scraps and snippets of paper.

"This has got to be it," Benny said, sitting in the wing chair. "He probably made the notes right at that desk there."

"The scene of the crime," Dominick said, nodding, and sat in the chair behind the desk.

Nonaka stood by the fireplace, scowling. He was beginning

to realize there'd be no damn doors to smash tonight; the knowledge was depressing and irritating.

"This is the first place I ever burglarized where I also sat down," Dominick said. "Usually, it's in, out, bingo."

"Only one thing to do now," Benny said thoughtfully.

"What's that?" Dominick asked.

"Go to Naples," Benny said.

"Right," Dominick said.

Benny nodded and reached into his jacket pocket. "Dominick," he said, "I am going to trust you to take this envelope to Ganooch's house in Larchmont, and give it to Nanny." He pulled one of the thick white envelopes from his pocket, fully realizing that he was handing fifty thousand dollars to someone who, by his own admission, was an experienced burglar, but figuring what the hell. "Tell Nanny may God help her in getting back that poor little kid from the maniacs that have got him," Benny said.

"Amen," Dominick said.

They walked to the front door. Nonaka suddenly crouched, shouted, "Hrrrrraaaaaaaaaaaaagh!" and gave the door a devastating shot with his right hand, splintering the wood near the lock. In the hallway outside, a woman in curlers opened her own door as they went past.

"What is it?" she asked.

"Vice Squad," Dominick said.

In the driveway of Many Maples, Luther and the boy paused before one of the rear windows, some three feet above the ground.

"That's it," Lewis said. "That's my bedroom."

"Are you sure?"

"Positive," he said.

"All right, I'm going to boost you up there," Luther said, "but first I wish to reiterate the terms of our agreement. You are not to tell anyone where you've been . . ."

"Okay," Lewis said.

"And you are not to reveal to anyone the identity of the people with whom you were staying."

"I wouldn't do that, anyway," Lewis said. "Ida's my friend."

"What about *me*?" Luther asked, offended.

"You?" Lewis said, and stepped into Luther's hands, and climbed over the sill into his room.

Bozzaris kept saying, "Uh-huh" into the telephone. He had been on the telephone from almost the moment he'd led Snitch into his office. Snitch assumed he was talking to someone at the lab, because whenever Bozzaris did not say "Uh-huh," he said, "But what about semen stains?" At last, he said, "Well, you work it out, I'll get back to you in the morning," and replaced the phone on its cradle. "Sorry to keep you waiting, Snitch," he said, "but first things first. In this corrupt and rotten city, we must deal with crime as it occurs, without favor or prejudice." He smiled broadly, put both elbows on the desk, laced his fingers together, and rested his chin on his hands. "Now then," he said, "what's this major felony you've got?"

"Does the twenty-five-dollar offer still hold?" Snitch asked.

"Of course."

"The major felony is a kidnaping."

Bozzaris opened his eyes wide and whistled softly. "Who's been kidnaped?"

"Carmine Ganucci's son."

Bozzaris whistled again. For the second time in as many days, the overpowering stench of money flooded into his nostrils and caught in his throat, almost causing him to gag. In all his years of experience, he had never heard of a kidnaping that did not involve a ransom demand. Nor was the kidnaping of Ganooch's son any small-time endeavor; the ransom demand here would undoubtedly be astronomical. Be that as it may, he thought, kidnaping and ransom demands alike are evil. It is my job to combat evil in all its slimy forms, and furthermore, to intercept any and all funds gained through evil means, which everyone knows are only earmarked for future evil undertakings. The roots, he thought. Strike at the roots, hack them away, and the mighty tree of corruption will fall, while simultaneously the squad's healthy and vigorous pension and retirement fund will spread its branches toward the beneficial rains of summer and grow to fruition perhaps sooner than expected.

"The information is worth twenty-five dollars," Bozzaris said.

"Thank you," Snitch said.

"You are a good man and a trusted adviser," Bozzaris said, opening the top drawer of his desk.

"Thank you," Snitch said.

"I hope you don't mind being paid in singles."

"No, that would be fine, thank you," Snitch said.

"We have been picking these up here and there around town during the past month," Bozzaris said, and handed a sheaf of bills across the desk.

"Thank you," Snitch said. He began counting the dollar bills, and then took a closer look at the top one, and squinted, and looked at it again, his telephoto gaze zooming in on the picture of General George Washington:

"Thank you," Snitch said glumly, thinking Crime does not pay.

*   *   *

In the living room at Many Maples, Nanny stared at the man with the stocking over his head and wondered how much longer she could stall him. She had already excused herself a total of four times, going into the kitchen and using the wall phone there to ring up Benny Napkins. Each time she had got only Jeanette Kay, who became increasingly more irritated because she was watching *Friday Night at the Movies,* and Nanny always called during a good part.

Arthur Doppio was very uncomfortable inside his stocking, but he supposed fifty thousand dollars was worth a little discomfort. He kept wondering when the Ganucci governess would come across with the money. All she kept doing, though, was asking him where the boy was, and then excusing herself all the time.

"Excuse me," Nanny said again, and rose, and walked swiftly out of the room.

Arthur figured she had a weak bladder.

"Can you please step on it?" Benny said to the cabdriver. "I have to catch a ten-o'clock plane."

"Plenty of time," the driver said.

"I'm supposed to be there an hour before departure."

"That's what they tell you," the driver said. "What they tell you is a lot of shit. You *don't* have to get there an hour before departure."

"I thought you did," Benny said.

"Hello?" Nanny whispered into the telephone.

"He's still not here," Jeanette Kay answered, and hung up.

Nanny sighed, carefully replaced the receiver on its cradle, and walked out of the kitchen. As she passed little Lewis's room, she glanced in and thought for a moment she saw the boy sitting up in bed, reading a comic book.

"Hello, Nanny," Lewis said.

Dominick drove very slowly because he was unfamiliar with Benny Napkins' little Volkswagen. Also, he did not have a driver's license, and he did not wish to get busted on some bullshit traffic violation. When he heard the police siren behind him, he thought for a moment that Benny had saddled him with a stolen vehicle. But the radio motor patrol car went speeding by on his left, its red dome light flashing, siren shrieking, streaking off into the night.

Dominick wondered what a New York City police car was doing up here in Westchester County.

He decided to drive even more slowly.

"You understand," the customs inspector said, searching, "that this is merely routine procedure, Mr. Ganucci."

"I understand," Ganucci said.

"We will very often make spot checks of citizens returning to this country."

"I understand."

"Taking them into this little room here, and stripping them down naked, as we have done to you."

"Yes, I understand," Ganucci said.

"Especially if we think they may be smuggling in heroin or diamonds or the like," the inspector said, probing.

Ganucci coughed.

"Out!" Nanny said. "He's back!"

"Who's back?" Arthur asked in terror. "Ganooch?"

"The boy!"

"Thank God!" Arthur said.

"Out!" Nanny said.

*   *   *

Coming up the driveway to Many Maples, Bozzaris passed a blue Plymouth sedan heading in the opposite direction. He turned quickly in his seat and caught a fleeting glimpse of the man behind the wheel.

"Is that a violation?" he asked his driver, a rookie who considered it a distinct honor to be chauffeuring the lieutenant.

"Is what a violation, sir?" the rookie asked.

"Driving a vehicle with a nylon stocking on your head?"

"Is that a trick question, sir?" the rookie asked.

"I don't know what this goddamn city is coming to," Bozzaris said, "pardon the French." He shook his head in deep despair. "People running around all over the place with stockings on their heads. I'm *sure* that must be a violation."

"Where did you wish me to park, sir?" the rookie asked.

"At the front door," Bozzaris said, "of course."

He got out of the car, walked up the path, and rang the bell under the *Ganucci* escutcheon, thinking all the while how unfair it was that an evil criminal like Carmine Ganucci could live in a beautiful mansion like this while he, Detective Lieutenant Alexander Bozzaris, lived in a two-family clapboard house in the Bronx across the street from a goddam junior high school.

"Who is it?" a woman's voice asked.

"Police officer," Bozzaris said. "Would you open the door, please, ma'am?"

The door opened. A woman in a black dress with a little white collar peered out at him and said, "Yes?"

"Detective Lieutenant Alexander Bozzaris," he said, and flashed the tin, which he knew in police jargon meant he was showing her his shield. "Upon information and belief," he said, "a major felony has been committed on these premises, which I am here to investigate."

"What major felony?" the woman asked.

"A kidnaping," Bozzaris said.

"Nonsense," the woman said.

"Upon information and belief," Bozzaris said, "the son of Carmine Ganucci was kidnaped Tuesday night. May I come in, please?"

"I am the child's governess," the woman said, "and he is in his bed reading a comic book."

"If that is true, may I please observe the alleged victim?"

"Follow me," the governess said.

Bozzaris followed her into the house, thinking, Look at this, look at the fruits of organized evil! Disgusting, a filthy materialistic ostentatious display, pardon the French.

"Lewis," the governess said, "this is Detective Lieutenant Alexander Bozzaris."

"How do you do?" Lewis said.

"Have you been kidnaped?" Bozzaris asked.

"No," Lewis said.

"Very well," Bozzaris said, thinking Crime does not pay.

As Dominick the Guru steered the. Volkswagen up the driveway to Many Maples, he passed a police car on the way out. He almost drove the small car off the road and into the trees lining the drive, but decided instead that this might look suspicious to any alert police officer. He drove to the oval in front of the house, cut the engine, and got out of the car. Standing in the driveway for several minutes, he listened with his good burglar's ears for the sound of the police car returning. Convinced that it had gone on its merry way, he rang the doorbell.

"Who is it?" a woman's voice asked.

"Dominick Digruma," he said, which was his proper name.

"Just a moment," the woman said, and unlocked the door. "Are you Nanny?"

"I am Nanny," she said.

Dominick reached into his pocket and handed her the thick white envelope. "This is from Benny Napkins," he said. "May God help you in getting back that poor little kid from the maniacs that have got him."

"Thank you," Nanny said.

"My pleasure," Dominick answered.

Nanny closed the door. Outside, she could hear Dominick's footfalls as he walked on the gravel toward his automobile. She heard the car starting, heard the tires squealing as he backed around, and then heard the engine gunning as he drove forward. The sound of the car receded. She waited until she could no longer hear it at all, and then she opened the envelope.

There seemed to be fifty thousand dollars in the envelope.

There also seemed to be a round-trip ticket to Naples via Rome.

Nanny grinned.

Benny Napkins was about to enter the Alitalia terminal when he suffered the fright of his life. A man, waving his arm at passing cabs, was striding along the sidewalk from the direction of the International Arrivals Building, followed by a big-breasted woman in a smartly tailored suit and a porter wheeling what appeared to be a dozen pieces of luggage.

The man looked exactly like Carmine Ganucci.

"Hey you!" he suddenly yelled at Benny. "Hey, Dummy!"

Benny stopped dead in his tracks. Whereas those had not been the exact words hurled at him in Chicago in the year 1966, when Ganucci had come there to upbraid him about the damage done to the goddamn window, the voice was unmistakable. Images of assorted mayhem, visions of drowning flashed through Benny's mind. In panic, he thought, Ganooch is home, he knows about the kid, and then prayed hastily and briefly to both St. Joseph and the Virgin Mother, begging that Dominick had been granted safe passage to Larchmont and that fifty thousand dollars' worth of insurance was already in Nanny's possession. Smiling numbly, his hand outstretched, he approached Ganucci and said, "Hey, hi! What're you doing *here*? Hello there, Mrs. Ganucci. I thought you were in Italy."

Without accepting his hand, Ganucci said, "What are *you* doing here?"

"I'm going to Naples," Benny said.

"What for?"

Benny lowered his voice. "To make a delivery," he said.

"To who?"

"To you."

"I'm here," Ganucci said. "Make the delivery here."

Benny reached into his jacket pocket, and handed Ganucci the second of the thick white envelopes, figuring that the fifty thousand dollars inside was being returned to its rightful owner, which was only fair. "Thank you," Ganucci said, "you done good." He transferred the envelope to his own pocket, and then turned toward the curb and yelled, "Taxi!" A cruising cab pulled up immediately. Ganucci stuck his head into the open window and asked, "You make out-of-town calls?"

"No, I don't," the driver answered.

"Yes, you do," Ganucci said, and opened the back door. "Come on, Stella."

In the living room of his West End Avenue apartment, Luther poured himself a drink and sat in the chair behind his desk. There were many things to think about, many things to ponder, least of which was the smashed front door—had he broken it himself in his frenzied haste to get the boy back to Larchmont? Well, no matter; he had already called the superintendent and been advised that the lock would be repaired in the morning. The super had also mentioned that it might be best to wedge a chair under the doorknob tonight because you never knew what kind of crooks were running around the city.

Luther sipped at his drink.

There was something to be gained from this entire experience, something to be savored and . . .

"Are you coming to bed?" Ida asked from the doorway.

"In a moment," he said, and then noticed that she was wearing the black nylon nightgown he had bought for her six years ago in Arnold Constable.

"Don't be long," she said, and turned and went out of the room.

Luther stared thoughtfully into his glass. There was no doubt in his mind that Ida had already benefited from the experience. Never before had he seen the maternal instinct so clearly revealed in man or beast. Once fermenting, who knew what such potent juices might brew? Would he himself become a father soon, protecting some helpless brood as fiercely as he had protected his kidnap scheme? The notion was not entirely fanciful; there was no question in Luther's mind that he had behaved admirably and bravely throughout, and that these very same qualities could be brought to bear on matters of less importance or urgency, as for example making Ida pregnant.

Luther walked slowly to the bookcase. His hand reached out for the cherished volume of Martin Levin reviews. He opened the book and scanned the pages leisurely until his eye fell upon a passage of exquisitely written prose, which he also considered germane to events of the recent past and immediate future:

The masculine mystique once again is prevalent here: courage, sacrifice, coolness, grace under pressure, and a hatful of other sidelines that are irrelevant except when they are needed.

He closed the book, replaced it on the shelf, and went back to his desk. Lifting his glass to the ceiling, he said aloud, "There's something for all of us to learn here. John? Martin? Malefaction does not yield recompense."

He swallowed the rest of his drink and went into the bedroom where Ida was waiting.

Jeanette Kay was already asleep when Benny got back to the apartment. He peeked in at her, and then went into the kitchen to fix himself a sandwich. Whereas Jeanette Kay did not like notes, she had left one for him on the refrigerator door, held in place there by a tiny daisy-shaped magnet. Benny took the note down and read it:

> Dear Benny,
> Nanny called again.
> She says thanks to your
> epics, the boy is home safe.
> Do not awake me as I
> am not in the mood for
> messing around with a
> bum who stays out all day.
> Your friend,
> Jeanette Kay

Well, Benny thought, at least *that* part is okay. The boy is back, thank God, and Ganooch will have nothing to get excited about. Except maybe the second fifty grand. He would have to try to find The Jackass in the morning. Somewhere out in the city, The Jackass was laying on a mattress wallowing in all that money, six thousand bucks of which was Benny's own. He would have to talk to The Jackass. He would have to patiently explain to him that even though the boy was returned and everything worked out all right, "Crimes are not to be measured by the issue of events, but from the bad intentions of men."

He made his sandwich, ate it, and went apprehensively to bed.

"Surprise!" Carmine Ganucci shouted.

"Surprise!" Stella shouted. "We're home, we're home! Where's Lewis?"

"In his bedroom, madam," Nanny said.

"Oh, I can't wait to see him!" Stella said, and took off her hat, and tossed it onto the hall table, and then rushed toward Lewis's bedroom at the back of the house.

"Hello, Nanny," Ganucci said.

"Hello, Mr. Ganucci," Nanny said.

"I took some nice pictures in Italy," he said.

"How nice," she said.

"Carmine!" Stella called. "Come say hello to your son!"

Ganucci went down the corridor to Lewis's bedroom. Stella was sitting on the bed, embracing the boy. Ganucci smiled. The kid, though no Cary Grant, looked more and more like him every day.

"How're you doing there, Lewis?" he said, and tousled the boy's hair, and then embraced him and kissed him on both cheeks.

"Great, Papa," Lewis said. "But I lost my watch."

"I'll get you a new one," Ganucci said, "what the hell."

"Did you miss us?" Stella asked.

"Almost," Lewis said.

"Huh?" Stella said.

"Well, we're home now," Ganucci said, "and it's great to be here. You know what I feel like doing, Stella?"

"What, Carmine?"

"I feel like developing some of those pictures I took in Italy."

"Now?"

"Now, Stella." He kissed his son again, said, "See you in the morning, Lewis," and walked out of the bedroom. Nanny was waiting for him in the corridor, near the kitchen. "Nanny," he said, "I want to develop some of those pictures I took in Italy."

"Now?" she said.

"Now. Do you think you could assist me in the darkroom?"

"Why, yes, Mr. Ganucci," she said. "Of course."

She followed him up the carpeted steps, walking behind him as she always did, and thinking of the fifty thousand dollars already tucked away in the bottom drawer of her dresser, not to mention the ticket to Naples via Rome which she could easily exchange for a ticket to London if and when life at Many Maples got too demanding. Madam Hortense, in fact, might be very happy to see her again.

"Carmine!" Stella called from the foot of the stairs. "Will you be developing film all night?"

"No, dearest," Ganucci replied, "just a roll or two," and opened the door, and graciously allowed Nanny to precede him into the darkroom.

18: NANNY

THE END

The author wishes to express his thanks and appreciation to the following good and honest citizens who posed for the various characters in this novel:

1: Richard A. Kennerson
(Graphic Designer)

2: Harry Melnick
(Retired Businessman)

3: Samuel N. Antupit
(Art Director and Publisher)

4: Richard Hunter and Mark Hunter
(Students, Harvard University)

5: Jack Farren (Theatrical and
Motion Picture Producer)

6: Charles F. Lombino
(Retired Mailman)

7: Robert Gage
(Art Director)

8: Dr. Fred Holtzberg
(Research Chemist)

9: Edward L. Lucci (Certi-
fied Public Accountant)

10: Evan Hunter
(Writer)

11: Ted Hunter (Student,
Silvermine Art College)

12: Gene Federico (Adver-
tising Agency Principal)

13: Jerry Bock
(Composer)

14: Ingram Ash (Theatrical
Advertising Representative)

15: Kaneji Domoto
(Architect and Landscape
Architect)

16: Stephen Antupit
(Photographer and
Sculptor)

17: Richard Condon
(Lieutenant, N.Y.P.D.)

18: Anita Ash
(Teacher)

The photo of Evan Hunter was graciously posed for by Ed McBain, the eminent novelist, author of *The Sentries* and other widely read books.

John Simon and Martin Levin are represented entirely by himself— themselves?—theirselves?—their own selves?—John? Martin?

The Martin Levin quotes on pages 32 and 33 are from the *New York Times Book Review,* 8/30/70.

The John Simon quote on page 33 is from *New York,* 9/7/70.

The John Simon quote on page 80 is from *New York,* 9/21/70.

The John Simon quote on page 171 is from *New York,* 11/30/70.

The Martin Levin quote on page 218 is from the *New York Times Book Review,* 11/15/70.

The ransom note on page 106 is composed of words clipped from John Simon's reviews in *New York* and Martin Levin's reviews in the *New York Times Book Review,* as follows:

"*This* type of interchange"—NYTBR, 11/29/70.

"is"—NYTBR, 11/29/70.

"factitious"—NY, 11/9/70.

"jaunty eclecticism"—NY, 11/9/70.

"(quite generous snippets, too)"—NY, 11/16/70.

"by"—NY, 12/7/70.

"a polymath"—NY, 11/16/70.

"The"—NY, 11/9/70.

"conspectus"—NY, 11/9/70.

"is cheerful and unassuming as a nosegay of wildflowers"—NY, 11/9/70.

"Let's put it this way:"—NYTBR, 11/29/70.

"you can go along with the rest of this buffoonery"—NYTBR, 11/29/70.

"or"—NY, 11/30/70.

"invite"—NY, 12/7/70.

"anfractuous"—NY, 12/19/70.

"unmitigated disaster"—NY, 11/30/70.

"roll back the tide of violence"—NYTBR, 11/15/70.

"enough money"—NY, 11/23/70.

"desiderated"—NY, 11/9/70.

"with"—NY, 12/19/70.

"oh-so-now"—NY, 11/9/70.

"delivery"—NY, 9/21/70.

"What we need immediately is"—NY, 8/17/70.

", though I shudder to mention it,"—NY, 8/17/70.

"lucrative"—NY, 8/3/70.

"capitalization"—NY, 8/3/70.

"Or"—NY, 9/21/70.

"will"—NY, 12/19/70.

"feel free to terrorize, foreclose and even murder."—NYTBR, 11/29/70.

The postcards on pages 14 and 98 and 99 are reproduced by permission of "Fotoedizioni Brunner & C.-Como."

The watch on pages 130 and 165 was created and copyrighted by Dr. Dougherty's Dirty Time Company, manufactured by Windert Watch Company.

All of the photographs in this book were taken by the author, with the exception of the picture of The Jackass on page 118, and the jacket photo, which were taken by Richard A. Kenerson. Mr. Kenerson also designed the jacket and devised the dollar bill on pages 59 and 211.

ABOUT THE AUTHOR

Ed McBain is one of the many pen names of legendary author
Evan Hunter (1926–2005). Named a Grand Master by the Mystery Writers of America, Hunter is best known for creating the
long-running 87th Precinct series, which followed an ensemble
cast of police officers in the fictional city of Isola. A pioneer of
the police procedural, he remains one of the best-loved mystery
novelists of the twentieth century. Hunter also wrote under the
pseudonyms Richard Marsten, Hunt Collins, John Abbott, Ezra
Hannon, Curt Cannon, and others.

ED McBAIN

FROM MYSTERIOUSPRESS.COM
AND OPEN ROAD MEDIA

   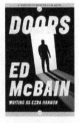 

  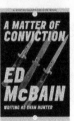 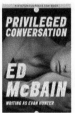 

MYSTERIOUSPRESS.COM

Otto Penzler, owner of the Mysterious Bookshop in Manhattan, founded the Mysterious Press in 1975. Penzler quickly became known for his outstanding selection of mystery, crime, and suspense books, both from his imprint and in his store. The imprint was devoted to printing the best books in these genres, using fine paper and top dust-jacket artists, as well as offering many limited, signed editions.

Now the Mysterious Press has gone digital, publishing ebooks through **MysteriousPress.com**.

MysteriousPress.com offers readers essential noir and suspense fiction, hard-boiled crime novels, and the latest thrillers from both debut authors and mystery masters. Discover classics and new voices, all from one legendary source.

FIND OUT MORE AT
WWW.MYSTERIOUSPRESS.COM

FOLLOW US:
@emysteries and Facebook.com/MysteriousPressCom

MysteriousPress.com is one of a select group of publishing partners of Open Road Integrated Media, Inc.

THE MYSTERIOUS BOOKSHOP, founded in 1979, is located in Manhattan's Tribeca neighborhood. It is the oldest and largest mystery-specialty bookstore in America.

The shop stocks the finest selection of new mystery hardcovers, paperbacks, and periodicals. It also features a superb collection of signed modern first editions, rare and collectable works, and Sherlock Holmes titles. The bookshop issues a free monthly newsletter highlighting its book clubs, new releases, events, and recently acquired books.

58 Warren Street
info@mysteriousbookshop.com
(212) 587-1011
Monday through Saturday
11:00 a.m. to 7:00 p.m.

FIND OUT MORE AT:

www.mysteriousbookshop.com

FOLLOW US:

@TheMysterious and Facebook.com/MysteriousBookshop

CPSIA information can be obtained
at www.ICGtesting.com
Printed in the USA
LVHW042031200319
611291LV00003B/108/P